"*Holding Court* somehow manages to be a charming and hilarious love story, while also being a spooky and twisty mystery. By the end, I couldn't tell if I was holding my breath more for how the mystery or the romance would play out. An amazing debut from an amazing author!" —Heather W. Petty, author of the Lock & Mori series

"Completely delightful—I didn't want it to end!" —Rachel Harris, *New York Times* bestselling author of *My Super Sweet Sixteenth Century*

"A rollicking romantic mystery bursting with delightfully quirky characters and unexpected revelations." —Katherine Longshore, author of the Gilt series

"I loved this fast-paced mystery filled with heart, humor, and Grayson's abs." —Talia Vance, author of *Spies and Prejudice* and the Bandia series

Holding Court

k.c. held

Entangled Publishing, LLC
2614 South Timberline Road
Suite 109
Fort Collins, CO 80525

Entangled Teen is an imprint of Entangled Publishing, LLC.

Visit our website at www.entangledpublishing.com.

Edited by Alycia Tornetta
Cover design by L.J. Anderson, Heather Howland,
and Kelley York
Interior design by Toni Kerr

Photos: Girl image (c) Early Spring/Shutterstock
Castle image (c) anpannan/Shutterstock
Stachoo/morguefile.com
gulden erikli tüllük/freeimages.com

ISBN 978-1-63375-227-6
Ebook ISBN 978-1-63375-228-3

Manufactured in the United States of America

First Edition March 2016

10 9 8 7 6 5 4 3 2 1

To Dan,
for believing in Someday

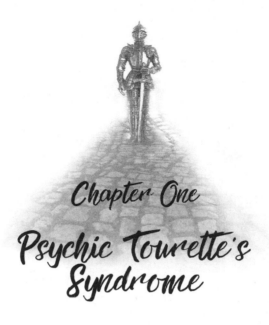

Chapter One
Psychic Tourette's Syndrome

I'm standing behind the counter of my mom's antique shop, thinking about Grayson Chandler's abs, when the bell over the door jingles and in walks Henry VIII.

"Uh, welcome to Love at Second Sight antiques. Can I help you?" I say.

"Greetings, fair maiden!" King Henry gives me a gallant bow. He looks like he stepped out of a painting. Or a psych ward. "I seek the proprietor of this fine establishment," he says, looking around at the various vignettes of period furniture, vintage clothing, and ephemera as he strides toward me. He spies the display case of antique weapons next to the front counter. "Ah, I see I have come to the proper place," he says, then reaches for the scabbard at his waist and unsheathes an enormous sword.

"Whoa," I say, taking a step back.

"'Tis a wondrous sight, is it not?" He laughs like he's auditioning to play Santa Claus at the county mall. He's still *ho-ho-ho*ing when the bell jingles again and Mom comes in carrying a bag from the deli across the street.

Gran pokes her head in from the back of the shop. She has packing peanuts stuck in her hair, which is currently dyed pastel pink, inspired by an episode of *America's Next Top Model*. "Is that lunch I hear? What took you so..." She trails off when she catches sight of King Henry. "Oh my," she says.

"I know, right?" I say.

"Can we help you?" Mom asks. She walks behind the counter, eyeing the sword King Henry is still holding aloft.

King Henry eyes my mom. She looks like a real-life version of Angelina Jolie (i.e. thirty pounds heavier and with discernible flaws), so she's used to being eyeballed.

"How interesting." Gran looks from King Henry to my mom and back again.

"Don't even," I say, knowing she's not referring to the fact that there's a guy dressed up like the former king of England brandishing a sword in the middle of our antique shop. I can tell by the way she's squinting at him that she's looking at his aura. And if she's comparing it to my mom's with that excited look on her face it can only mean one thing.

"*Stop that,*" Mom hisses under her breath, making shooing motions behind her back. She knows what Gran is doing, too, and it's making her blush.

King Henry is still smiling, although he's begun to look a bit confused. The women in my family tend to have that effect on people. The only thing that could possibly make the situation more awkward would be for me to have one of my uncontrollable psychic fits.

So, of course, I do.

"The keeper of secrets keeps too much!" I blurt, then clap a hand over my mouth.

King Henry looks like he's waiting for the punch line.

"Indeed," he finally says.

"Is there something we can help you with?" Mom asks. She shoves the bag of sandwiches at Gran. "Why don't you take your lunch break? Now."

Gran nods, still squinting at King Henry. "Fascinating. An almost perfect match," she says as she backs through the velvet curtain behind the front counter.

"Milady," King Henry says to Mom, and lays the sword on the counter, "I seek your expertise in the matter of my sword."

"How so?" Mom asks. She picks up the weapon, balancing its weight in both hands.

"I am told it is a sixteenth-century German sword, and I wish to verify its authenticity, for I do not trust the blaggard who sold it to me."

"Well, I would say the blade is certainly mid-sixteenth century."

I know Mom knows *exactly* how old it is but she probably can't be too precise without making King Henry suspicious.

"But the hilt is a later addition. Probably a Victorian reproduction," she says.

"Bloody hell!" King Henry roars and pounds a giant fist on the counter.

Mom gives him "the look."

"Pray pardon me, your ladyship." I swear King Henry actually blushes. "Are you certain?" he asks.

"I'm certain," Mom says as she tilts the sword back and forth under the lights. "If it makes you feel any better, it's a beautiful reproduction. It might even be one of Ernst Schmidt's, but you'll have to take it to someone who specializes in his work to know for sure."

King Henry nods and takes the sword from her, replacing it in his scabbard. "Alack, I feared it might be so," he says. "Thank you, milady. Next time I shall seek your counsel before I am foolish enough to exchange coin for counterfeit."

"May I?" Mom reaches toward the thick gold necklace he wears over his elaborate costume.

"'Tis the only surviving chain of office from the time of His Majesty, Henry VIII," King Henry says as he leans forward. At least he knows *he's* not Henry VIII.

Mom wraps her fingers around the necklace and closes her eyes. "Mmm," she says, "how lovely."

When she opens her eyes, their faces are inches apart and I'm about to barf.

"Just in time!" I blurt and they both stare at me. "Uh, Cami's here," I explain, except she isn't. "I mean, she will be. You know, any second now." I'm saved from further explanation by the jingling bell.

"Hey, Jules," Cami says when she sees me, and then she takes in King Henry. Without missing a beat she drops into a curtsy, setting her corkscrew curls bouncing. "Your Highness."

King Henry gives her his gallant bow and says, "Please, rise, fair maiden."

"You must be the Tudor Times dude," she says. "Nice duds."

"Many thanks," King Henry says, then turns back to Mom.

"Is there anything else I can help you with?" she asks.

"No, milady. I thank you for confirming my suspicions. Prithee forgive me for my outburst. In faith, I should not have been surprised."

Mom reaches for his other necklace and I'm about to tell them to get a room when she says, "You do know *this* is a reproduction, I hope?"

King Henry nods. "Verily, I commissioned it myself."

"It's a pity they didn't use genuine stones, it's such a beautiful piece."

"Pardon?" King Henry looks down at the pendant, his face starting to turn purple.

"Oh, dear." Mom lets go of the pendant and takes

a step back. "You didn't know?"

"I most certainly did not," King Henry says. "By my troth, I fear I am an even bigger fool than I thought. Tell me, milady, might I compel you to come to Lunewood Castle to look upon the rest of my collection? It seems I could use someone with your practiced eye."

"I'd love to," Mom says, looking all excited, and then she sighs like a punctured blow-up doll. "Unfortunately I'm leaving tomorrow to do some appraisal work in Europe. I won't be back for several weeks."

"I am unsurprised that a lady of your talents is in high demand," King Henry says and reaches for her hand. He brushes his lips across her knuckles and says, "Perhaps another time?"

"Your nun is pregnant!" I blurt.

Everyone stares at me, and I decide my best option is to make a dash for the back curtain.

Gran looks up and sees my wide eyes and my hand over my mouth. "What'd you say this time? A real doozy, huh?"

"I can't... I don't even... Gran, I think it's getting worse."

"You probably just have more to say," Gran says. She's annoyingly prosaic about my bizarre outbursts.

Cami comes through the curtain behind me and lets out a snort of laughter. "Way to ruin the moment, Jules." She grabs the bag of sandwiches and holds it up to her forehead. "Let me guess, smoked turkey on sliced sourdough?" She peeks in the bag. "Yes! I'm totally psychic, too!"

"Shut up," I say and grab the bag from her. "I hate you."

"Do not."

"Do, too. Oh, crap."

"What?"

"Nothing."

"Tell me!"

I hold my breath and clamp my lips together.

"Out with it, Blurt."

I shake my head furiously.

"You can't possibly hold it in, so you might as well tell me before you burst a blood vessel."

I blow it out in one big breath. "You're going to get the lead in *My Fair Lady* and Sidney Barlow is going to tell everyone you cheated."

"Dude," she says. "Seriously?"

"Yes. And stop calling me Blurt."

"I'm going to get the lead? That's awesome! And Sidney Barlow can suck my Chucks." She gives me a quick hug. "I'm going to go work on my monologue. Call me when you get off work!"

*S*ince Mom had decided to accept the appraisal gig in Europe, and refused to take me with her, and my dad was off on another one of his archaeological digs, and refused to take me with him, I was doomed to spend another boring summer in Lunevale helping Gran plant begonias. And since Mom couldn't trust either of us in the antique shop in her absence, I was also officially out of a job for the summer. Again. Not that Mom gives me very many hours to begin with.

I'm only allowed to work when her assistant, Dee, isn't working. Dee is high-fructose-corn-syrup sweet and has the IQ of a dust bunny, but the customers love her and she always knows exactly what to say to get someone to buy a $10,000 Fabergé ashtray. A talent I do not possess. Mostly I help unload stuff and attach price tags. Occasionally I get to do something really challenging like dusting bric-a-brac.

Mom tries to use me at the front counter as little as possible on account of my tendency to yell out things like, "Your maple has tar spot!" and scare away the customers. But she's my mom so she's never actually fired me. Not even after the time I told Dee her underwear was on fire. Even though it was (dryer malfunction).

Despite being founded by Lucius Lune, who definitely outranked me and everyone else in town on the Freak Scale, the rest of Lunevale is not so forgiving. In its present-day state the inhabitants of my hometown fall into three basic categories: the inveterate townies whose families have been here forever; the hipster refugees from the San Francisco Bay Area in search of better schools, a lower cost of living, and their own version of quirky small-town America; and the visiting tourists who provide most of Lunevale's livelihood.

The townies are used to eccentrics like Gran and the Lunes and old Mr. Farley (otherwise known as the Corpse). It's mostly because of hypocritically intolerant hipsters and skittish tourists that I've been fired from every job I've ever managed to land. Which isn't very many, since interviews are stressful and stressful situations tend to set off what Cami calls my "Psychic Tourette's Syndrome." Which means I rarely make it through an interview without blurting out something bizarre or alarming. But since my PTS has yet to help me predict the winning lotto numbers—because that would actually be useful—I desperately need a new job. Like, yesterday.

Chapter Two
Tudor Times

One of the reasons I so desperately need a job is so I can buy a car, but since I don't have a car there are only so many jobs I can get to. It's a tragic paradox that could seriously scar my entire high school career.

"It has to be something in Lunevale," I tell Cami the next morning when she barges into our kitchen and finds me looking through the help wanted ads in the local paper. Cami lives next door and spends as much time as possible at our house in order to avoid her own family, which is inordinately loud and exuberant. Much like Cami herself, who, according to Gran, has more dazzle than a disco ball. Mom and I moved into Gran's huge, old, Pepto-Bismol-pink Victorian after my parents' divorce and have been here ever since. My dad stayed in San Francisco and is usually too busy digging up mummies to be a decent dad. He's way more interested in dead people than he is in the living. Which is probably why my mom left him, despite the fact that he has this whole Indiana Jones thing going on.

"I have to be able to get there on my bike or the bus," I say. "Since having your driver's license obviously means nothing around this place." I give Mom a pointed look. She actually *laughed* when I asked if I was getting a car for my sixteenth birthday.

Mom puts down her coffee and looks at her watch. "I'd better go finish packing. I'll be at the shop most of the day. I need to go over a few things with Dee before I leave tonight." She kisses me on the head and goes upstairs.

Gran lowers her *People* magazine. "You're welcome to use Rosie," she offers.

Cami and I look at each other, and I roll my eyes. Rosie is a major part of the reason I need a job in the first place. I refuse to drive my grandmother's hot-pink golf cart to school next year.

"Uh, thanks, Gran, but I think I'll pass on the golf cart."

Gran huffs and looks offended. "Rosie is not a golf cart, she's a Neighborhood Electric Vehicle."

"What's the difference? She still can't go on the highway."

"Suit yourself. You can take the back roads, you know."

"I'd *have* to take the back roads, Gran. Rosie only

goes twenty-five miles per hour."

"Well, what do you need to go faster for? No one can read my signs if you go too fast."

Did I mention that Rosie, the hot-pink golf cart, is plastered with ads for Gran's matchmaking business, An Aura of Romance?

"And you can park right up front in those special electric vehicle spaces like they have at the Target."

"Tempting, but I'd rather risk the sweaty helmet hair and ride my bike." Helmet hair or hot-pink golf cart. I seriously need a car, ASAP.

"No way!" Cami grabs my highlighter and circles an ad. "Check it out, there's a listing for Tudor Times. And it couldn't be more perfect." She holds up the newspaper.

> HELP WANTED: Do you have the gift of visions? Tudor Times, Candor County's newest must-see destination, is looking for a dynamic, outgoing individual to add to our Castle Team. We're currently seeking a female performer to portray the character of the Maid of Kent. Duties include wearing an appropriate period costume and performing psychic readings for Castle Guests. No experience necessary.

I look at Cami. "You're kidding, right?"

"Come on, it's like it was written for you! You can do your Psychic Tourette's thing without having to worry about getting fired. Plus that King Henry guy is the owner and he obviously has the hots for your mom, so you know he's going to hire you."

"He's not going to hire me, because there's no way I'm applying for it."

Instead of arguing with me, Cami whips out her phone and punches in a number. "Hello, I'm calling about your ad in the *Lunevale Gazette*?"

I make a grab for the phone, but she jumps off her chair and backs away, wiggling her fingers at me. "Yes, I'm very interested in the psychic job. One thirty? That would be perfect. My name's Juliet Verity. I'll be there at one thirty. Thank you so much."

"What the hell?" I say to Cami after she hangs up.

"You'll thank me for this, trust me." Cami gives me a smug grin and sits back down. "A bunch of kids from Lunevale High are working there this summer."

"So?"

"So, one of them happens to be Grayson Chandler."

"And?" I feign total indifference, but the truth is the mere mention of his name gives me palpitations.

Cami closes the newspaper and starts counting on her fingers. "Number one, you need a job. Number two, Grayson Chandler. Number three, you finally get to see the inside of Lunewood Castle, and number four, you get to dress up in a fancy Tudor gown that is bound to give you fabulous cleavage. Ergo, you're an idiot if you don't take the job."

"Number one"—I hold up a finger, too, the

middle one—"I do not have the 'gift of visions,' I have an involuntary blurting disorder, which, in case you've forgotten, is something I've been trying to suppress for years. Number two, Grayson Chandler has a girlfriend, and do I really need to remind you of my history with Grayson and castles? Number three, if I want to see the inside of Lunewood Castle all I have to do is buy a ticket to Tudor Times. And number four, I don't think it's possible for me to have cleavage regardless of what I'm wearing."

"Whatever. You know you want to see Grayson dressed up like a knight, looking all Prince Charming." She gives me a wicked grin. "I bet he has a really big sword."

"Oh, shut up. I hate you."

"I believe my work here is done. I'm out. Don't forget, one thirty. Say hello to Prince Charming for me!"

"Well, that sounds promising, dear," Gran says, looking up from her perusal of the red carpet trend report. "It's about time you put your talents to good use. And I'm not talking about the cleavage." She waggles her eyebrows at me.

"Seriously? You think I should take a job giving fake fortunes to a bunch of tourists at a cheesy castle?"

"Who says they have to be fake?"

"In case you haven't noticed, I don't exactly have control over my 'gift,' Gran."

"No, you don't have the ability to shut it off. You might be able to learn some control if you embraced your gift instead of trying so hard to tamp it down."

"Embrace what? All I ever do is blurt out ridiculous, meaningless, or crucially embarrassing stuff. Why would I want to do that more often? I get into enough trouble as it is. I've been fired from every job I've ever had, including my volunteer job at the library—which is beyond pathetic—been suspended from school for my outbursts in class, and, depending on how you feel about circus sideshows, am considered either a freak or a hilarious spectacle by the population at large. It's not a gift. It's a curse. Why can't I do something that's actually useful like you and mom?"

"I suppose that depends on how you define 'useful.'"

"Oh, whatever. I'm going to go pout in my room."

I flop down on my bed, pull on my headphones, and choose something appropriately morose to listen to. Then I close my eyes and find myself imagining Grayson Chandler in tights. Something I've done probably daily since he moved to Lunevale five years ago. Which isn't as weird as it sounds since he showed up for the first day of school in a *Princess Bride* T-shirt and he had the same floppy hair and shy smile as Westley, the hottest tights-wearing farm boy/pirate in cinematic history. When Grayson turned out to be as funny as he was dreamy, I was a total goner. So was almost every other girl at Lunevale Elementary.

On the day I finally summoned up the guts to talk to Grayson, I ended up getting suspended from school. It was a misunderstanding involving a math test and one of my psychic flashes, but Grayson has avoided me like the plague ever since. He also happens to have the most perfect girlfriend in the world, so there's no way he'd be interested in me even if I weren't a total freak. Bree Blair is so perfect you can't even hate her properly.

And while Grayson purposely avoids me, Bree goes out of her way to be nice to me. When we were younger, she never made fun of my uncontrollable outbursts and gave hell to any kid who did. She once made Josh Gaddis eat his Batman eraser after he snuck up behind me in the cafeteria, yelled, "You're going to use a number two pencil when you take your test today!" and made me spill chocolate milk down the front of my favorite sweater. She'd been one of my best friends until about seventh grade. Which is when things got super awkward. As Bree was blossoming into the most popular girl in school, I was becoming a candidate for biggest freak. Plus it was torture to watch Grayson gaze at her so adoringly; everyone else was clearly extraneous when they were together.

So, yeah, the only thing worse than being in love with someone who is in love with someone else, is being in love with someone who is in love with someone else who is a thousand times more perfect than you can ever hope to be.

But despite the utter lack of romantic possibilities, I am apparently incapable of passing up the chance to ogle a tights-wearing Grayson Chandler from afar, because just before one thirty I find myself cursing Cami under my breath as I pedal into the staff parking lot at Tudor Times.

Chapter Three
The Maid of Kent

I find a place to lock my bike and attempt to revive my helmet hair before reporting for my interview. I've never been inside the famed Lunewood Castle before, although I snuck onto the grounds once with Cami on a dare. Up until last year it had been owned by old Mrs. Lune, whose husband's grandfather had the castle shipped over stone by stone from his ancestral homeland as a gift for his bride. The whole marriage thing hadn't turned out so well for the original Mr. Lune, who was rumored to be a pervy nutjob, but the castle was pretty amazing.

Old Mrs. Lune had come into my mom's antique shop once, but I'd scared her off when I blurted something about not being afraid of alligators and hot pants. Mom was seriously peeved, considering how much money Mrs. Lune has to spend on Fabergé ashtrays.

Anyway, after refusing offers from interested buyers for years, last year Mrs. Lune had suddenly decided to retire to Florida. She sold Lunewood Castle to Hank Bacon, aka King Henry, an über-wealthy Tudor fanatic who, according to the internet research I'd done in preparation for my interview, had made his millions by inventing some sort of hemorrhoid gel. Hank apparently had a thing for Henry VIII and thought everyone else should, too, because he'd decided to turn Lunewood Castle into a Tudor-themed tourist attraction.

Tudor Times had opened a few months ago, and the citizens of Lunevale were pretty much split down the middle on how they felt about it. The half that liked the idea saw job opportunities and tourist dollars; the half that didn't griped about the fact that the castle had been bought by a nutcase with a Tudor obsession. But since "nutcase with a Tudor obsession" also described the original Mr. Lune, I'm not sure what all the fuss was about, especially since most of Lunevale gets off on being Quirky Town, USA. Plus, Hank Bacon had opened the castle to anyone who was willing to pay the price of admission, whereas the Lunes had been notoriously snooty.

All *I* want from Tudor Times is the chance to make some money and to ogle Grayson Chandler from afar. And possibly wear a sumptuous gown that gives me awesome cleavage.

Lunewood Castle sits on a hill overlooking Lune Valley and is everything you'd expect a castle to be, right down to the lily pads floating in the moat. I follow the hedge-lined gravel path that leads from the parking lot to the rear of the castle and pass a small courtyard in which a bunch of sweaty guys in tights are thwacking each other around with wooden practice swords. As I'm craning to see if one of them is Grayson, I run smack into someone's sweaty chest.

"Excuse me, milady," Sweaty Chest says, grabbing my arms to keep me from falling.

I look up at his face and make a sound between a whimper and a sigh. It's Grayson Chandler, and he looks like he just stepped out of one of my *Princess Bride* fantasies. His brown hair is perfectly tousled, and he has on a flowy white shirt with a slit down the front that exposes his chest and a hint of his infamous abs. I look into his mesmerizing green eyes and instead of saying something spectacularly witty like, "Is that your sword or are you just happy to see me?" I blurt, "The Hepplewhite hides the boogers!" Then I tear myself out of his grip and run the rest of the way to the castle without looking back.

I pull open the door marked SERVANT'S ENTRANCE and take a second to catch my breath. I'm leaning over with my hands on my knees when an enormous pair of embroidered white leather Mary Janes steps into my line of vision. I look up to see a crusty old guy dressed in a red uniform with a poufy skirt and white tights giving me the eagle eye. He only has one; the other is covered with a black leather eye patch.

"May I be of service, milady?"

"Um, sure," I say. "I'm Juliet Verity. I have an interview at one thirty for the Maid of Kent position?"

"Maid of Kent, eh?" he says. "So, she finally got caught, what-what?"

"Pardon me?"

"You'll be wanting to go to the King's study, Mistress Verity. The stairs are at the end of the hallway." He points me in the right direction.

"Thanks, uh..." I pause, waiting for him to tell me his name.

"Floyd. Floyd Bean. But most folks call me the Keeper."

"Okay then, uh, Mr. Bean...Keeper. I'd better get to my interview." I have the sudden feeling of pressure in my head and chest that tells me my PTS is about to strike. I bolt for the stairs, anxious to get away from the Keeper and his creepy one-eyed stare before I say something I'll more than likely regret.

"Was there something else, Mistress Verity?"

I shake my head, but it's too late. "Stop, or you'll feel the maiden's embrace!" I yell.

I don't wait for the Keeper to respond.

When I get to the second floor, a woman in a beautiful Tudor gown directs me to Hank's office. I knock on the heavy wooden door and a booming voice responds, "Prithee enter!"

I open the door to find King Henry sitting behind a large wooden desk. He's using an old-fashioned feathered quill to write something, but puts it down when he sees me.

He looks at me with some surprise and, I think, confusion. "Mistress Verity?" he says, reaching a hand up to scratch his robust beard.

"That's me, uh, Your Majesty," I'm not sure what the protocol is so I drop a curtsy and then feel stupid for doing so. I'm wearing a vintage 1950s polka-dot dress I found on the last thrifting trip I went on with Mom. With my Bettie Page hair and cherry-red lip gloss, I stick out like a sore thumb in Lunewood Castle. But then, so does the laptop I spy on the corner of Hank's desk. I'm not sure what the Tudor equivalent might be. An abacus?

"Please, be seated, Mistress Verity. Am I to understand you are interested in portraying the Maid of Kent?"

I nod.

"I must confess, I believe a few curious things are now beginning to make sense."

"Oh?" I have no idea what he's talking about.

"The fact that you have the gift of visions. Or do you know Angelique personally?"

"Angelique?"

"The current Maid of Kent, the woman whose position you would be filling while she is on maternity leave."

"Oh, uh, no. I've never met her. I've never been to Tudor Times before, actually."

"Indeed? Then I suppose we can dispense with the question of your abilities."

"We can?"

He grins at me. "I believe you proved yourself in

your mother's shop. How is Lady Anna, by the way? It was indeed a pleasure meeting you both yesterday."

"She's getting ready to leave for Paris. Which is why I'm out of a job for the summer."

"I see. Do you have any experience performing in front of large groups? Your duties as the Maid of Kent would include being part of the dinner entertainment for the castle guests."

"Oh. Um, I went to theater camp in junior high?" I don't tell him that, against my better judgment, Cami had coerced me into signing up, and I'd blown my first audition when I burst a blood vessel in my eyeball trying to keep myself from blurting that Sidney Barlow was going to start riding the crimson wave in the middle of the balcony scene in *Romeo and Juliet*. I ended up being given the job of prompter. I was supposed to follow along in the script and help the actors if they forgot their lines. Which is a ridiculously inappropriate job for someone with a blurting problem. I'd lasted one dress rehearsal.

"Fair enough. Why don't we start you out on a trial basis? Angelique will give you a tour of the castle and go over the position with you. I suggest you shadow her for a day or two and then see if you're ready to try your hand at it. You will be provided with an appropriate costume as well as a dossier on your character. I ask that you keep all evidence of the twenty-first century hidden from the castle guests. If you have a cell phone, please store it in your assigned cupboard in the Great Wardrobe at the beginning of your shift. What do you say, Mistress Verity? Shall we start you today?"

"Um, it sounds great but...I feel like I should warn you that my, uh, 'gift of visions' is kind of unpredictable. Sometimes...well, really, most of the time, I blurt things out without meaning to and they're not always...what people want to hear," I confess.

"Not everyone wants to know what their nun is up to, eh?" he says, then throws his head back and does his Santa Claus laugh.

I'm starting to think he's completely bonkers when I remember my blurt from yesterday.

"I warrant you will do just fine, Mistress Verity. Lucky for you, the Maid of Kent was a total nutter. The guests will assume anything you say is part of the show." He stands up and reaches for the ornate pocket watch hanging from a chain around his waist. "Now if you will excuse me, I must prepare for today's guests. You'll find the Great Wardrobe downstairs in the southeast corner of the castle. Tell Geoffrey, the Master of the Wardrobe, you are to be the new Maid of Kent. He will provide you with a costume for today." He steers me toward the door. "Once you're dressed, you can report for duty in the Oratory on the upper floor of the Rose Tower. Good luck, Mistress Verity."

"Uh, thanks, Your Majesty. See you around," I say and scurry out the door.

I make a clandestine phone call to Gran to let her know I'm giving the Maid of Kent thing a go and won't be home for a while. Then I make my way downstairs and through the winding stone hallways to the costume shop, aka the Great Wardrobe, where I meet Geoffrey. He's immaculately dressed in a white Tudor-style jacket with lace at the neck and sleeves, and huge poufy red pants that resemble a pair of scarlet pumpkins. He's also sporting a low ponytail, a black leather fanny pack, and an enormous pair of scissors.

I tell him who I am and he puts down the scissors. He grabs a tissue and hands it to me. "Lose the eyeliner and the lip gloss. You need to look as natural as possible." He watches while I wipe off the offending makeup, then goes to one of the wooden cupboards that line the far wall. He rummages inside, then hands me a folded stack of black fabric and points me toward one of the curtained stalls that serve as dressing rooms.

"It's pretty self-explanatory. Get dressed and I'll show you how to do the wimple."

"Um, okay," I say. What the hell is a wimple?

"Just holler if you need help," he says, and I pull the dressing room curtain shut.

I take off my polka-dot dress, then unfold the pile of black fabric and discover a T-shaped black dress with an extra flap of fabric over the chest in the front and another in the back. "Um, I think there's been a mistake," I call to Geoffrey. Where the hell is my cleavage-inducing Tudor gown? I knew this job sounded too good to be true.

Geoffrey yanks open the dressing room curtain and I drop the black sack dress and try to cover my bra and underwear with my arms. I start to get that weird feeling of pressure that means I'm about to have a PTS moment. In my underwear, in front of a strange man I've just met. "The cabbage is only the beginning!" I yell and wait for Geoffrey to respond since there's nothing else I can do. He's blocking my exit and, oh yeah, I'm in my underwear.

Geoffrey stares at me, and I can almost see him decide to go with pretending I haven't said anything. Which tends to be the most popular choice of people I verbally assault. He looks down at the crumpled black dress.

"Oh, I forgot to give you a shift. Hang on."

He disappears and comes back a moment later with a long white nightgown-looking thing that he gathers up and plops over my head. I stick my arms into the sleeves as the fabric falls to my ankles. He picks up the pile of black linen. "The scapular's attached, so the whole garment goes on at once," Geoffrey says, and over the shift it goes. He finishes adjusting the dress and I turn to look at myself in the mirror. I look like I'm wearing a tent, complete with a door flap in front.

"Wow," I say. "Aren't I supposed to wear a sumptuous gown or something?"

"For the Maid of Kent? Hardly. What size shoe do you wear? I'll get you some boots. You're not allergic to wool, are you?"

I shake my head, still trying to process what I'm seeing in the mirror.

"Good. You'll need stockings and a leather belt,

and then I'll show you how to attach the wimple and veil."

Even before I see the wimple I'm fairly certain I'm going to kill Cami for coming up with the whole Ogle-Grayson-Chandler-From-Afar scheme.

She could not have been more wrong about both the cleavage and the gown I will be sporting. To my utter mortification I discover that the Maid of Kent was a *nun*.

Chapter Four
Your Nun Is Pregnant

The first person I see as I step out of the costume shop, in my full-on nun ensemble, is the impossibly gorgeous Bree Blair. She's dressed up like a Tudor queen in a fabulous gown that gives her the kind of cleavage it would take a Miracle Bra for me to achieve.

Seriously? As if my life didn't suck enough right now?

"Jules! What are you doing here?" She envelopes me in a rose-scented hug. She doesn't just look perfect, she smells good, too. I should hate her. But I can't.

"Uh, hi. I didn't know you were working here. How...awesome?"

"I know, right? When did you start? Oh, how fun!

Are you the Mad Maid of Kent? That's so perfect!"
She somehow manages to say this and sound sincere
instead of insulting.

"Um, yeah. Today's my first day. King Henry
hired me on a trial basis."

"Oh, you'll be great! Isn't this wild? I never
thought I'd get to see the inside of this place. But
here I am. Don't you love my gown?" She grabs her
skirts and spins around in a circle. "I get to play
Catherine Howard. She was Henry VIII's fifth wife.
I'm learning so much about Tudor history. It's totally
fascinating, don't you think?"

"Yeah, totally," I say.

"You haven't seen Grayson, have you? He was
supposed to bring me his car keys."

"Um, I saw him outside a while ago," I say and
realize I would rather die than run into Grayson while
dressed as a nun. "Yeah, so, good luck, but I have to
go, uh, have the gift of visions." And then my head
is filled with the image of Grayson's sweaty chest
inches from my own and I am no doubt blushing
furiously as I blurt out, "Durst the truth for the lady
who waits!"

"Sorry?" Bree responds.

"Yeah, I have no idea what that means," I say.
"Just ignore me and my brilliant flashes of nonsense."

"You're too funny, Jules," Bree says, but she
doesn't look all that amused. "I'd better finish
getting ready." I'm certain she's finally decided I'm
too weird to waste her time on when she reaches out
and squeezes my hand. "I'm so glad you're working

here. It's been way too long since we've had a chance to hang out. And this is such a perfect job for you." She gives me a wink, and then she's gone in a rustle of scarlet silk and heaving bosoms.

I practically sprint for the Oratory, which is where the Nutty Nun of Kent apparently has her visions, in an attempt to avoid running into Grayson, or anyone else I might know. I'm uncomfortably sweaty by the time I reach the door to the room where I get to hang out and be ogled by tourists. I use the front flap of my tent dress to wipe the sweat off my forehead before pulling open the heavy wooden door.

Inside the octagonal room, another woman in a nun outfit is standing with her back to me, talking on a cell phone.

"I know. He said this is a family establishment and he can't have the 'younger castle guests' asking about pregnant nuns." She pauses. "I *know*. I've got maybe two more weeks, but still. It freaking sucks. I don't know how he found out. It was probably Sarah, she's always up in everyone's business. If she ratted me out I'm going to—"

The woman whirls around and I finally put it together. *Your nun is pregnant.*

"I have to go," she says into the phone, then shoves the contraband device under the front flap of her dress. She looks like she's only a couple of years older than me, and she's wearing her nun outfit without a belt, so I probably wouldn't have noticed otherwise, but now that I *do* know, I can see the way her tent dress poofs out a little too much in the front.

"Who are you?" she demands.

"Jules," I say, holding out my hand, "Jules Verity."

"Well, Jules Verity, I guess you're the lucky girl who gets to take over my job while I get transferred to the gift shop," she says and shakes my hand, gripping it a little too tightly. "I'm Angelique Boden, the pregnant nun."

"I'm really sorry," I say. "I had no idea."

She waves a hand. "Not your fault."

This is debatable, but I decide against telling her I was the one who told King Henry his nun was pregnant. Instead I blurt out, "Endure the boots or face the doom!"

She gives me a funny look, then lifts the hem of her dress. Her painfully puffy-looking feet are sporting metallic purple toe polish and chunky black Doc Martens sandals decorated with silver spikes. Definitely not de rigueur nun wear. "You've obviously never been pregnant. There's no way I can fit my feet in those boots at this point, and I fricking hate those itchy stockings. I'm allergic to wool. So Geoffrey can suck his insistence on 'authenticity.' What are you, some kind of costume Nazi?"

"No. I, uh, I didn't mean... It's none of my... The stockings *are* really itchy. I'm sure you... I like your shoes. The metal spikes add a really nice touch." I give her a thumbs-up.

"Okay, then." She takes a seat at the carved oak table pushed up against one of the stone walls. The room is beautiful, all Gothic arches and stained glass windows. Next to the table is a heavy wooden chest flanked by iron candlesticks holding fat, flickering candles. On the opposite wall a large embroidered pillow sits on the colorful tile floor in front of an altar tucked inside a small alcove.

"There's a character dossier in the chest there. Why don't you pull it out and I'll give you the lowdown on the Mad Maid of Kent. I have a feeling you'll fit right in."

I assume she's referring to the "mad" part. "I wasn't really expecting the nun part," I say.

"Me, either." She leans back and gives her belly an affectionate pat. "Pull up a chair, sister."

I open the wooden chest and retrieve a leather portfolio featuring an engraving of a young woman lying sprawled on the steps of a church.

"That's our girl," Angelique says, pointing to the picture. "Elizabeth Barton, otherwise known as the Mad Maid of Kent. Basically she was a servant girl who got sick and started raving like a lunatic. Then a bunch of priests decided she had the gift of prophecy and told her she should become a nun. So then everyone thought she was this fully legit prophetess and came to see her and hear about her visions and it was all hunky-dory until she pissed off King Henry and he had her executed."

"Nice."

"Yeah. So, anyway, you get to hang out in here and pretend to have visions when the tourists come through on their tour of the castle. And then you give a performance in the Great Hall during dinner. Don't worry, I'll walk you through it all."

"Thanks, that'd be great. So, um, what are you going to do now that you can't play the Maid of Kent?"

"I get to work in the gift shop until I explode. And Hank's offered me six weeks of maternity leave, but I doubt I'll come back after I have the baby. I like the gig, but Lunevale itself is so not my scene."

"Tell me about it."

"You grow up here?"

I nod.

"How old are you, anyway?"

"Sixteen. And I desperately need a car so I can do something besides ride my bike around Quirky Town, USA."

She laughs. "I remember being your age. Just got your license?"

Uh-oh. Blurt alert. "Augustus arrives with that which you seek!" I yell in her face.

"What?"

"Sorry," I say. "I didn't meant to—"

"Who told you to say that?"

"What? No one. I have a blurting problem. It happens more when I'm nervous. Like now. My friend Cami calls it Psychic Tourette's Syndrome. PTS for short. I call it mortifying."

She narrows her eyes at me. "You mean you're actually psychic?"

"Not really. Most of the stuff I say doesn't make any sense. But sometimes it's more specific. I know it's annoying and everything, but I don't know how to stop it and— I'll just stop talking now."

"Interesting."

"Wait a minute," I say. "Aren't *you* psychic?"

"You mean, do I have the 'gift of visions?' Hell, no."

"But how do you do readings and stuff for people?"

"Jules, honey"—she leans forward as far as her belly will let her and takes my hand—"you're pretending to be a batshit crazy psychic nun from the sixteenth century in a castle owned by a guy who's obsessed with Henry VIII. How much credibility do you think is expected here?"

"Uh, yeah. Good point."

"That said, you can make a killing on tips if you read people right. It's the best part of the gig, moneywise. And you don't have to have the gift of visions to read people, you just have to be a quick study."

"What does that actually mean?"

"It means when someone walks in you do an assessment, decide on what tack to take, and start talking. You can tell from their body language if you're on the right track. It's easy once you get the hang of it. You ever heard of Miss Marple?"

"As in, Agatha Christie's *The Body in the Library* Miss Marple?"

Angelique nods. "See, Miss Marple has this theory that the world is made up of certain types of people and once you figure out what type someone is, you know almost everything you need to know about them. Let's take you for instance."

"Um, let's not?"

"Oh, come on, it'll be fun. I'll pretend I'm giving

you a private reading so you can see what it's like. I'll do you and then you can do me."

"I liked it better when all I had to do was act batshit crazy."

She laughs. "Okay, I'll walk you through a typical day first. Once you're in costume, you come up here and one of the pages will bring you the schedule for the day. If you don't have any private readings scheduled, you leave the door open and act nunly while the castle guests troop through on their tours. You pick one or two people from each group to do premonitions for. Nothing fancy, just a line or two. Then, once everyone is seated in the Great Hall for dinner, you head over to the minstrel gallery and spy on the guests while they're waiting for the show to start."

"Okay, you lost me. I'm supposed to *spy* on people?"

"Only if you want to get the good stuff. There's a big wooden balcony halfway up the wall in the Great Hall where you can stand and listen in on everyone down below. Once I've got something I can use for the show, I go downstairs. King Henry and his wives do their thing and sit down for dinner, the jester does his thing, blah, blah, blah, and then King Henry calls you over and asks if you have any visions to report, and you do your crazy nun shtick and make a prediction about someone in the room and King Henry asks if any of the castle guests can verify if what you say is true, and if you've done your job right, someone will jump up all breathless and excited and

you look like a psychic genius and King Henry thanks
you and you're done for the night. Easy, right? You
can stay up in the gallery tonight and watch me do
my thing. Sound like a plan?"

"Sure," I say, but I feel panic welling up inside
me. Or maybe it's another blurt. Sometimes I can't
tell the difference.

"Good. Now I'll show you what I do for the
private sessions. Let's pretend you just sat down for
your reading." She clasps her hands together, bows
her head and murmurs something under her breath.
Then she looks up at me and gives me a beatific smile.
"Welcome, my child. What can I help you with?" She
speaks in a quiet, soothing voice that sounds nothing
like the no-nonsense one she was using a few seconds
ago.

"Um, I was hoping you could do that whole
psychic thing?"

"Of course, of course. Give me your hand, my
dear, and let us see what we can find out about your
future."

She sounds totally earnest and concerned and
it's not hard to pretend she's an actual nun.

"What I need you to do is to remain open and
relaxed so that you can receive whatever messages
come through." She smiles at me and takes my other
hand. Then she winks and says in her normal voice,
"Okay, I've set the scene, given you an idea of what
to expect, and encouraged you to go along with me.
Now I'm going to tell you the things I know from
observing you. You're female, above average looks,

sixteen years old, Caucasian, brown hair and blue eyes, tall and slender. You have sensitive skin but you take very good care of it, you have a scar above your left eyebrow, no evidence of smoking, drug taking, or alcohol use. Unfortunately I can't tell you anything about your clothes since you're all nun-ed up, but you have no visible tattoos, your ears are pierced once each, you have no discernible accent, and your hands are clammy."

"Wow," I say as I pull my hands away from her and wipe them on my dress. "Sorry about the sweaty hands."

"No worries. Okay, now that I've Miss Marpled you and settled on a preconceived stereotype, I'll focus the reading on areas that are generally of concern to people like you. I.e. romance, school, friendships, family, etcetera. Then I'll say a bunch of stuff that seems to pertain specifically to you but could really apply to anyone."

She takes one of my hands again and looks at me earnestly. "You don't have a boyfriend but there is someone you're interested in. Someone who's unattainable or refuses to acknowledge you exist. You generally like school, but sometimes have trouble fitting in. You feel like your parents aren't being as supportive as they could be, and that frustrates you. Now I pause and wait for you to confirm my statement."

I nod my head.

"You have strong feelings for someone but it's a complicated situation and you're not sure what to do."

"Um, how do you know that?"

She laughs. "Honey, you're gorgeous. If you don't have a boyfriend, you should."

"Uh, thanks," I say, and try not to blush.

"You've just started a new job and are feeling uncertain as to whether or not you're up for the challenge it presents."

"Ha, ha."

She drops my hand and starts laughing. "Sorry, couldn't resist. Okay, if you're having trouble coming up with stuff for someone you can always fall back on the crazy nun persona. Like so." She moans and puts her hands to her veil as her eyes roll up into her head. She mumbles something unintelligible that sounds like it might be in Latin. Then she focuses on me again and says, "I will try to pass on this message, but it is difficult to translate and you must help me decipher its meaning." She shivers and grabs my hand. "Mistress Verity, you have considerable unused talents that the spirits urge you to take advantage of. Do you understand this message?"

"Um, I guess so," I say. I know she's messing with me, but it's still kind of unnerving to a have a nun staring at you and pretending to whisper urgent messages from the spirits. "I'll, uh, work on that."

"You shouldn't be so critical of yourself, Mistress Verity."

"I know, but—" I clamp my mouth shut. I can't believe I'm actually falling for this shtick.

"All right, Jules. Relax. I'm making this stuff

up. Now I'm going to do what's called 'fishing.'" She leans forward. "Your parents divorced when you were a little girl?"

I try not to respond at all.

"Aha! You just gave yourself away."

"What'd I do? And how did you know that?"

"Your left eye twitched. And it was a lucky guess, plus the odds are in my favor. Okay, so, the other thing you can do is phrase your questions using the negative. No matter how the person responds, you can act like they're confirming your statement. Let's try it: You're not an only child, are you?"

I nod.

She nods back. "I thought so. Now if you'd said, 'No, I have ten brothers and sisters,' I could have made the same response and acted like you were just confirming what I already suspected. Get it?"

"You're not married, are you?" I say, and she looks surprised for a moment, then laughs.

"Very good, you're a quick study."

"This is all making me kind of uncomfortable. Can't I just mumble a bunch of stuff in Latin and call it a day?"

"Not if you want a big tip."

"People actually tip you?"

"Absolutely. Are you kidding? That's what makes the whole thing worth it. This job doesn't pay enough without the tips. Okay, so I think you get the picture. If you ever have a reading that's going south, you want to have a couple of 'outs' that you use. If someone is obviously not buying your spiel you can say something like, 'You must open your heart to these messages, my dear.' Or, 'The spirits are doing their best, but you must try harder to make sense of their messages.' You can always blame the spirits. 'The messages are not very clear today,' or, 'The spirits are finding it difficult to come through today,' whatever. *Capiche?*"

"Got it."

"You can also use drama or flattery to spice things up. You know, roll your eyes back in your head and mumble a few Latin phrases, yada yada, tell them they have soulful eyes, blah, blah, blah. Sometimes people simply want someone who will listen to them. In those cases you just do a lot of nodding and smiling."

I nod and smile.

"Then at the end you wrap it all up in a way that makes you seem like a psychic genius." She leans toward me, an earnest expression on her face. "What the spirits want you to take away from all this is that your mother and father love you very much, even though they often seem wrapped up in their own problems. This new job you've started is going to be a really positive thing for you, you're going to form new friendships and tap into some of those special talents you need to take advantage of. And that boy you're in love with, things are going to be shifting soon. Don't give up hope. You have some strong support from the spirit world, they're watching over you and will help you succeed. Thanks for letting me pass on these messages today. It was a pleasure meeting you,

Mistress Verity." She squeezes my hand and I swear
she's tearing up. Then she says, "I'm starving. Grab
me a Snickers out of that chest, would you?"

Chapter Five
There's Our Victim

I spend the next couple of hours watching Angelique do her thing for the tourists. If I didn't know better, I'd swear she was actually psychic. She does three private readings and by the third one I'm starting to see the things she sees and then uses in her readings. It's like she's part detective, part therapist, and by the end of her sessions the castle guests are in awe of her "gift of visions." The response is completely contrary to the one I usually get for sharing *my* "gift," and it leaves me feeling a little giddy.

When there are no private readings scheduled, we sit and act nunly while the tourists troop through in small groups led by a costumed Tudor character. Angelique picks someone out of every group to target and make some sort of premonition for. There's lots of gasping and nudging from the crowd, and eye-rolling, Latin-spouting overacting from Angelique.

Once the last group has filed through, Angelique leads me into the hallway and over to a small door set opposite the Oratory. I duck through the door after her and find myself on a narrow set of steps leading down to yet another door. This one opens out onto a sturdy wooden balcony overlooking the massive Great Hall below. There are several heavy wooden tables set in long parallel rows running lengthwise down the room, and at the front of the Hall, another table set crosswise upon a raised stone dais where, judging from the huge throne-like gold and velvet chair in the middle, King Henry and his entourage will sit.

A trumpeter dressed in red and gold takes his place at the front of the room and plays a short burst of music to announce dinner. Angelique and I stand quietly and watch the tourists file in. They wander around the Hall, gazing at the sumptuous decorations and talking animatedly before choosing their seats.

Angelique nudges me and points to a woman directly below us who's clutching her companion's arm and looking around wide-eyed at the beautiful tapestries, stained glass windows, and enormous carved stone fireplace.

"Oh, it's perfect!" she squeals. "We have to get married here!"

Her companion grins down at her and pats her

left hand, which sports a large diamond engagement ring on the third finger.

"There's our victim," Angelique whispers as they take their seats. "I'll head down in a minute. You can stay up here and watch the show. Meet me back in the Oratory after I finish my premonition."

The trumpeter plays an elaborate fanfare, and a procession led by an attendant carrying a large red velvet cushion enters the Hall. The attendant places the cushion on the throne at the front of the room and bows as King Henry takes his seat. He has all six queens with him, including Bree, as well as his noble knights. As the queens' ladies-in-waiting and the knights' squires bring up the end of the procession and take their seats among the tourists I finally get my chance to ogle Grayson Chandler from afar. He looks every bit the Prince Charming as he marches in carrying a banner for one of the knights.

I tear my eyes away from Grayson to focus on the banquet proceedings. Servants enter carrying trays of food. Roast beef and salmon, chicken and sausages, huge slices of bread, plates of cheeses, piles of vegetables, and an assortment of desserts including puddings, fruit and custard tarts, and little marzipan animals that look too cute to eat. As the people load up their plates, the sound of bells announces the arrival of the court jester, who grabs several wheels of cheese off the table and proceeds to juggle them over the guests' heads. They duck and cringe, and he cracks jokes and pokes fun at King Henry and his queens and makes everyone laugh.

Then a pair of acrobats come tumbling into the room, doing flips and contortions that make the tourists gasp.

King Henry and the woman playing his first wife, Catherine of Aragon, act out a brief dramatic scene in which they announce the birth of their daughter, Mary. Everyone pretends to celebrate, and the servants bring the guests mugs of wine or grape juice to toast with.

When everyone settles down to eat their dessert, King Henry says, "Ah, I see the Holy Maid of Kent has a message for us."

Angelique comes forward and bows to the king. "If I may have a word, Your Majesty. I have had a most interesting vision that I believe concerns one of your guests."

"Indeed," King Henry booms. He gestures at the crowd of tourists. "Well, let us have it, Sister Elizabeth. What is this grand vision of yours?"

Angelique turns to face the crowd, closes her eyes, and puts her hands to her veil. "I see a bride. She is a wee slip of a thing, pale blond with an ethereal beauty. She wears a white dress with a long flowing train." Angelique opens her eyes and walks slowly toward the center of the room. All eyes are on her. There are some stifled giggles, but mostly the crowd seems to be eating it up.

Angelique holds out her arm, gesturing toward the huge wooden doors at the back of the Hall. "I see her now, she walks toward me, a radiant smile on her face." She turns back to the raised dais. "And there is her prince," she points to a space to the right of King Henry. "He stands, his heart swelling with joy as he waits for his lady, his love, to become his wife." Angelique suddenly sinks to the floor and the crowd gasps. Two young men dressed in Tudor uniforms rush to her and grasp her beneath the arms, lifting her gently to her feet.

"So beautiful," Angelique stage-whispers into the stunned silence. "They will be so happy together."

I search out Angelique's "victim" from the faces in the crowd. As the two men lead Angelique out of the Hall, the blond woman turns her head to watch and I see the moment when their eyes meet. There are tears streaming down the young woman's face as Angelique gives her a beatific smile. "You will be so happy," Angelique says as she disappears from view.

The young woman looks up at her fiancé, and he leans down to kiss her tenderly on the lips.

I'm still wiping tears away when I meet Angelique back in the Oratory.

"Do you think that was too much?" she asks. "I laid it on a little thick." She's out of breath, and the look in her eyes reminds me of the sculpture of an ecstatic nun I saw in one of my mom's art books. Or possibly Jack Nicholson in *The Shining*.

"Wow. That was intense," I say.

"It's the hormones. I get a little carried away. Don't worry, people are equally impressed when you predict their kid is going to win his soccer game. And that's a day in the life of the Mad Maid of Kent. Think you can handle it?"

"I guess so."

"Oh, come on. You have the added bonus of actual psychic ability. Do you know how jealous I am? Just think of all the awesome things you can yell to freak out the tourists."

"That's what I'm afraid of."

"Again, you're playing a crazy psychic nun. I think anything's fair game. Now, let's go get some dinner before the hordes descend." Angelique starts for the door and then stops, putting a hand to her chest. "Hold on a sec, my phone's ringing." She reaches under the front flap of her dress and pulls out her cell phone.

I reach my hand under my own flap. "These things have pockets?"

Angelique laughs. "Where else would you keep your Bible?" she looks down at her phone. "I need to take this. I'll meet you in the staff dining room." She puts the phone to her ear and makes shooing motions at me. I hear her say, "Yeah, it's done," and then the door swings shut behind me.

Since I don't know what else to do with myself, I go in search of the staff dining room.

Chapter Six

Oh. Jeez. She's Dead

’ve just entered the main hallway on the
ground floor when I hear voices coming from
somewhere down the wide stone hall in front
of me. I would know one of the voices anywhere. It
belongs to none other than Prince Charming himself,
Grayson Chandler. Without thinking, I duck into
an alcove to my left that holds a suit of armor. I'm
trying to squeeze between the suit and the wall when
my elbow bumps the handle of the ax held aloft by
the armored glove. The ax drops forward, there's a
loud grating sound, and the little circle of stone I'm
standing on starts to turn.

An opening appears in the wall behind me and
I give a yelp of surprise and panic when I realize
I've triggered some sort of secret entranceway. The

stone circle grinds to a stop and I find myself in total darkness. I stand still for a second, trying to get my bearings, then put my hands out and take a step forward, feeling for something solid in the darkness around me. I turn slowly until my fingers come into contact with the suit of armor. I shift slightly to my left and run my hands over the rough stone wall to the side of the alcove, searching for a light switch or a doorknob or something that will either help me figure out where I am or get me the hell out. I reach higher on the wall, and my hand brushes against something that feels like a post set inside a metal bracket. I run my fingers along the post until I find a small knob at the top. I hold my breath and twist the knob.

There's a soft *click* and a wall sconce flares to life. I step back from the sudden glare and stumble over something lying on the floor behind me. I do a kind of hopping chicken dance as I try to regain my balance but end up landing on my elbow on the hard stone floor. My eyes fill with tears from the sharp pain in my arm and I lie there for a second trying to decide if my elbow is broken or just missing the top layer of skin. Once I determine it's bloody but functional, I sit up, and that's when I see the girl lying on the floor staring up at me.

"Oh, jeez, I'm sorry," I say. "I didn't mean to step on you, I had no idea anyone was in here. Um... are you okay?" She doesn't say anything, just stares at me with these bulgy bloodshot eyes, and then I notice the chain wrapped around her throat, biting into her skin. "Oh, crap. You're dead, aren't you?"

When she doesn't answer, I reach a finger out and touch her forehead. She doesn't respond. I let out a whimper and scramble backward. And then I hear something in the passageway behind me. Something that sounds like heavy breathing.

I stand up and throw myself at the suit of armor. "Help!" I scream. "Someone get me out of here!" I run my fingers over the stone wall again, searching for a mechanism that will open the secret entranceway. I hear a scraping sound behind me and I scream again. I grab for the ax, desperate for something to protect myself from whoever, or whatever, is in the passageway behind me. Instead of coming free, the ax tips forward and the circle of stone begins to move again.

I'm still screaming when I find myself back in the main hallway, face to face with Grayson Chandler and a guy holding a very large sword. Before I can stop to think, I throw myself at Grayson, burying my face in the folds of his billowy white shirt.

"Grayson! Oh my God, there's a girl in there. And she's dead!"

He grabs my shoulders and gently eases me away from him.

"Jules? Is that you?"

I nod and look down at his lovely white shirt. There's blood on it. "Oh, jeez. I'm sorry," I say. My elbow is worse than I thought, there's blood running down my forearm and onto my hand.

"Is that blood? Holy crap, are you okay?"

"Yeah, I scraped my elbow when I tripped over the dead girl."

"What? Jules, what are you talking about? Where did you just come from?"

I point to the alcove behind me. "I was trying to hide behind the suit of armor and I accidentally triggered some kind of secret opening and all of a sudden I was in this passageway. I tripped over something and it was this girl and I thought she was just lying there for some reason but she was *dead*. Then I heard a noise and that's when I started screaming and I went to grab the ax so I could protect myself but the door thingy opened again and, oh my God, we have to call the police!"

"Okay, Jules, take a deep breath. Why don't you come over to the stairs and sit down?"

He leads me to some stone steps and I sit, my whole body shaking. He crouches down in front of me so that we're eye to eye.

"I'm going to send my friend Drew here"—he motions to the guy with the sword—"to get King Henry."

"I'm on it," Drew says. He slides the sword into the scabbard at his waist and takes off down the hallway.

"Okay, tell me again about the girl you saw." Grayson says. "Are you sure she was dead?"

"I'm sure. She was very, very dead."

"What did she look like?"

"She was young, maybe a few years older than me. I think she had brown or black hair and dark eyes. And, oh my God, she was dead, Grayson. She was just staring at me and I—"

He puts both hands on my shoulders, "It's okay, Jules. It's going to be okay. Take a deep breath."

I nod and clamp my knees together so they'll stop shaking.

"I'm going to go check the passageway, okay?"

"No! There was someone else in there. I could hear them breathing. What if it was whoever killed that girl? And they're crouched in there, waiting for someone to—"

"Okay, we'll wait for reinforcements. How's your arm. Is it still bleeding?"

"I think it's okay. I'm sorry about your shirt."

"Let's take a look," he says and reaches for my hand.

I've only imagined Grayson Chandler holding my hand about fifty million times and now that the moment is here...it is both everything and nothing like I'd imagined. His hand feels warm and sure, and I have a couple of seconds to focus on the sensations it's sending throughout my body before they're eclipsed by pain and I try not to wince as he gently pulls back the sleeve of my nun costume.

"That's quite a scrape. You've got a nasty cut as well. It's still bleeding a bit. I'm going to hold your arm up and put some pressure on the cut, okay?" He pulls the sleeve back down and lifts my arm over my head, squeezing it gently.

"Thanks. You're good at the whole first-aid thing." And the being-gorgeous thing.

"Lifeguard training. I was planning to get a job at the community pool this summer until I found out Tudor Times was hiring. No contest, right?"

I'm thinking I'd *very* much like to see a contest between bathing suit–wearing Grayson and tights-wearing Grayson.

"Um, Jules? If you don't mind my asking, what are you doing here, anyway?"

I gesture at the nun getup with my free hand. "Oh, you know, the usual." I flash back to the girl in the passageway and make this crazy strangled laughing sound.

"The usual?" Grayson looks more than a little concerned.

I take a deep breath and try to tamp down the hysteria. "How did I end up stumbling over a dead body in a secret passageway while dressed as a nun? Um, it's a long story. The short version is, I was just hired as the new Maid of Kent."

"Oh. Whew. For a second there I was worried you'd actually taken vows or something."

"Vows?"

"To become a nun." He grins at me, and I wish he would look at me like that every single day for the rest of my life. "You're taking over for Angelique? I didn't know she was quitting."

"She, uh, has a conflict of interest."

"How come you're not working in your mom's shop?"

"My mom's doing some appraisal work in Europe this summer, so her assistant's running the shop.

And I, uh, make her assistant nervous."

"Gotcha. Well, her loss is Tudor Times's gain. Although I'm not sure you're having such a great first day."

We both look over at the suit of armor.

"So, um, you're a knight, huh?" I say, not wanting to think about what lies beyond the secret entrance.

"I wish. I'm what's known around here as a 'squight.' Technically I'm a squire who's training to be a knight, but even though I know all the routines by heart I can't be a knight until I turn eighteen. Which means I only get to joust and battle bad guys when I'm done cleaning up horse poop. It's all very glamorous."

"It has to be more glamorous than being a nun. So what do full-fledged knights get to do?"

He reels off a quote from *The Princess Bride*, "'Are you kidding? Fencing. Fighting. Torture. Revenge. Giants. Monsters. Chases. Escapes. True love. Miracles.'"

"'It doesn't sound too bad. I'll try and stay awake.'"

Grayson presses a hand to his heart. "Did you just quote my favorite movie back to me?"

"Do R.O.U.S. live in the Fire Swamp?" I can't contain the grin that takes over my face as I realize I'm sitting with Grayson Chandler, trading *Princess Bride* quotes. It's like my most fervent sixth-grade fantasy has suddenly come true. If you ignore the dead body, the bloody arm, and the nun costume.

"How now! What is the meaning of this?" a loud voice demands and I look around Grayson to see

King Henry barreling down the hallway with Drew trailing behind him.

Grayson and I both stand, and King Henry comes to a stop and looms over us. The guy must be at least six and a half feet tall.

"Sir Drew has been bending my ear with a preposterous account of a body in a secret passageway. Prithee explain yourselves."

I point to the alcove. "It's in there."

King Henry looks at my hand. "Is that blood, Mistress Verity?"

"Yeah, I hurt my arm when I tripped over the girl in the passageway."

"I see." King Henry steps over to the alcove, looks at the suit of armor, then back at me. "Mistress Verity, you do know the show is over for tonight? If you are trying to convince me of your ability to play the Mad Maid of Kent, I assure you, your efforts are in excess. May I suggest you save your psychic visions for the castle guests?"

"This wasn't a vision, Your Majesty. I was, um, standing in the alcove and I triggered something that made that little stone circle spin around." I point at the faint circular outline on the floor. "There's a passageway on the other side. And there's a dead body in it." I shudder as I try to shake off the image of the dead girl staring up at me.

"Pish! Show me," King Henry demands.

"It's right on the other side of the wall. If you tilt the ax down I think it triggers some kind of mechanism."

King Henry steps toward the suit of armor.

"But I think there's someone else in there. Someone... not dead. I didn't see anyone, but I definitely heard what sounded like heavy breathing before I freaked out and grabbed the ax and ended up back out here."

"I see," King Henry says and in one quick motion he draws his sword. "Then I shall bring something to greet them with."

Chapter Seven
Well. This Is Awkward

King Henry holds his sword at the ready with one hand as he pushes the ax down with the other. He's so huge he barely fits on the stone circle with the suit of armor. "By Saint George, how did I not know of this?" he says as it begins to spin, and then he disappears into the secret passageway beyond.

Grayson, Drew, and I exchange looks.

"Do you think we should follow him?" Drew asks.

"*I'm* not going back in there," I say. "I don't have a sword." Not that I would go back in if I did have one.

"I'm pretty sure he can take care of himself," Grayson says.

There are no panicked screams from King Henry,

but then *he* was expecting to see a dead body. We wait in silence, all eyes on the wall where the suit of armor has been replaced with a curved section of stone. If I didn't know about the revolving alcove, I would've never noticed the very faint outline between the stones.

After what seems like endless hours later, the wall begins to move and King Henry reappears.

He gives me a strange look and re-sheaths his sword.

"Nothing in there but cobwebs," he says.

"What?" I ask, certain I must have misheard him.

"There is no body," King Henry says. "Nothing but an empty passageway with a staircase at either end."

"But that's impossible," I protest. "She was right there on the other side of the wall. I saw her."

King Henry shakes his head. "I do not know what you saw, but there is nothing there now, Mistress Verity."

"I swear there was a dead girl in there. Why would I make something like that up?" I take a step toward the alcove and stop. I don't want to go back in there, but I can't believe the body is gone. There's no way I hallucinated a dead girl. Is there? "She was lying in the middle of the passageway, to the left of the suit of armor? Brown hair, dark eyes. She had a thick gold chain wrapped around her neck?"

"I assure you, Mistress Verity, the passageway is quite empty. Perhaps you were mistaken about the"— he pauses as if searching for the right word—"*vitality* of the girl you saw."

"There's no way she was alive. I think someone strangled her. Her eyes were bulging out of her head and her face was all purple and—"

King Henry holds up a hand. "You are welcome to check the passageway yourself, Mistress Verity."

I look at King Henry and then the alcove. "You didn't hear anyone else in there? What if they're hiding? What if I go in there and..."

"I'll go with you," Grayson says, looking at King Henry for approval.

King Henry nods and Grayson steps onto the stone circle and holds out his hand. "It'll be a tight squeeze but I think we can both fit."

I take his hand and join him on the stone circle. We stand with our faces inches apart, our bodies pressed together. I bite my lip and reach for the ax, fear and uncertainty over what I saw in the passageway distracting me from the thrill of being this close to Grayson Chandler.

He puts one hand on my shoulder and the other on his sword hilt. "Ready."

I push the ax and we spin into the passageway beyond.

There is no girl, dead or otherwise.

"She was right there." I point at the bare stone floor. "I swear, Grayson. She was lying there with her eyes open and the chain wrapped around her throat and she was dead. Absolutely and completely dead."

"I believe you, Jules," he says, but I can't tell if he means it. He looks up and down the passageway. "I wonder where the staircases lead."

Before I can stop him he takes off down the passageway. I hurry after him and we come to a stop at a set of stairs that spirals upward.

"These look like they go to the second floor. Do you know what's above us?" I ask.

"I'd guess King Henry's private rooms. They're off-limits to the staff. Let's see where the other set goes."

We walk to the other end of the passageway where we find a narrow set of stairs leading down into the dark.

"What do you think is down there?" Grayson asks.

"The Pit of Despair?" I suggest.

Grayson gives a nervous laugh. "There must be a light switch somewhere," he says, running his hand along the wall at the top of the stairs.

"I'm not going down there."

"Yeah, we definitely need a light."

"Or a lobotomy." I look back down the secret passageway toward the suit of armor. "If there are stairs leading to other parts of the castle, that means there are probably other entrances to the passageway, right? So there definitely could have been someone else in here with me when I found the body."

"On second thought," Grayson says, looking down the dark staircase. "Maybe we should finish this conversation back in the main hall?"

"Good plan," I say. "You believe me, don't you? I swear I didn't hallucinate a dead girl."

"I believe you," he says, but avoids looking at me.

We step back onto the stone circle and his face is once again inches from my own. He smells like peppermint soap, fresh hay, and boy. If I leaned forward a little bit and he tilted his chin...

"Well, this is awkward," Grayson says, grinning down at me.

"The cuckoo favors another nest!" I blurt, and want to pull my wimple over my face.

Grayson looks like he's considering cuckoo things, too, as he reaches out and tilts the ax.

Once we're back in the hallway I'm expecting Grayson to tell King Henry what a nutjob I am, but all he says is, "You're right, Your Majesty. There's no sign of a body in there."

King Henry looks pissed. "Mistress Verity, please report to the Great Wardrobe to turn in your costume. And get that arm taken care of. When you are finished please come to my study."

"Yes, sir," I say.

"I will deal with this," he says to Grayson and Drew, then he reaches out and yanks the ax out of the armored glove. "In the meantime, this passageway is off-limits. Understood?"

We all nod, and King Henry waves the ax at us. "Off with you now. And not a word of this to anyone."

Everyone nods again, but if King Henry thinks no one's going to hear about my dead body hallucination, he's crazier than the Mad Maid of Kent.

*A*s I round the corner to the Great Wardrobe I run smack into Floyd "the Keeper" Bean.

"Well, hullo, Mistress Verity," he says, "or should I say, Sister Elizabeth?"

"Uh, hi," I say and try to step around him.

"I hear you're the new psychic nun. Have you a premonition for the Keeper?"

"What? No. Sorry. Listen, I need to get changed and—"

"Why so hot and bothered, Sister?"

Um, ew. "You know, you're really good at that leering thing. Is that part of your character description or is that your own personal touch? It's very charming in an I'm-a-voyeuristic-taxidermist-loner kind of way," I say because it's much easier to be irritated by Floyd at the moment than it is to think about the dead body I may or may not have just imagined.

"Ah, a feisty one. I like it."

Oh, please. "Yeah, well, don't get too attached. I'm probably about to get fired. Now, if you'll excuse me." I push past him and make a break for the door of the Great Wardrobe.

"I'll be watching you, Sister. That's the Keeper's job, you know," Floyd calls after me as I duck through the door.

Geoffrey looks up as I enter the shop. "Is everything all right out there?" he asks, "I thought I heard some sort of commotion in the hallway."

"Yeah, I, uh, I thought I saw something but it was nothing. Everything's fine." I grab my clothes from my cubby and make a beeline for one of the dressing rooms.

"What did you think you saw?" Geoffrey asks as he follows me over to the dressing room.

"I wish I knew," I say as I pull the curtain shut in his face.

I wrestle with the pins holding on my veil, then strip off the rest of my Maid of Kent outfit and pull on my polka-dot dress, careful not to get any blood on my clothes. When I come back out Geoffrey is still standing right outside the dressing room.

"Uh, hi," I say.

"You're bleeding."

"Yeah, do you have any Band-Aids?"

Geoffrey retrieves a first aid kit from one of the cupboards and hands it to me. "Blood is very difficult to remove from linen," he says.

"Yeah, sorry about that." I hand him the wad of nun clothes. "Hopefully it's only on the sleeve of the nightgown thingy and not the dress, too."

"Habit."

"Pardon?"

"It's called a habit. The garment worn by the Holy Maid of Kent. There's the habit, and attached to that is the scapular. Underneath it you wear a shift and on your head you wear a wimple and a veil."

"Good to know," I say, but he just stands there looking down at the wad of clothes in his arms while I clean the blood off my arm and slap a giant Band-Aid on my elbow.

"King Henry is very particular about these things.

Everything must be historically accurate down to the smallest detail."

"Yeah, well, right now King Henry is waiting for me in his study, so I'd better get a move on."

"Yes, of course. Mustn't keep His Majesty waiting. You know what happens to those who displease Henry VIII." He smiles, so I'm pretty sure it's meant as a joke, but I'm too fresh from my dead body experience to find it the least bit amusing.

As I'm climbing the stairs to the second floor, I think about the fact that King Henry went into the passageway by himself. And I realize he was probably in there long enough to get rid of a dead body. He could have hauled it up the stairs to his private rooms or tossed it down the stairs or...

I stop outside the door to King Henry's study, suddenly nervous about losing more than my job as a psychic nun at a cheesy tourist attraction. Just how far was Hank Bacon, Tudor superfan, willing to go to get into character as Henry VIII, a guy who hanged or beheaded anyone who pissed him off?

As a precautionary measure, I pull out my cell phone and dial Gran's number. When her voicemail picks up I whisper into the phone, "Gran, it's Jules. Just so you know, I'm about to go into a meeting with Hank Bacon, aka King Henry. If I don't come home tonight tell the police to look in the secret passageway. There's an entrance behind the suit of armor in the main hallway on the ground floor. I love you. Bye."

I stick the phone back in my backpack, take a deep breath, and knock on the heavy wooden door.

Chapter Eight
Should Have Seen That Coming

"Have a seat, Mistress Verity," King Henry says when I enter the room. He's sitting behind his desk, still in costume. "How are you feeling?"

"Like I'm about to be beheaded for treason? I'm not really sure how to answer that question."

"Nervous? Confused? Scared? I would think one or all of those would apply. Mistress Verity, I will be honest. This is a new one for me. I have never had an employee, psychic or otherwise, claim to see a dead body that then disappeared before anyone else could verify its existence. I hardly know how to proceed. What does one do under these circumstances? Call the police? Close the castle and have it thoroughly searched? Take a head count and make sure all of my employees are accounted for? Contact all of the visitors who came to the castle today and make sure they left with the same number in their party that they came with? Do you see the quandary I'm in? I do not wish to alarm anyone, but at the same time the safety of my employees and that of the castle guests is of the utmost importance to me. As I am sure you understand."

"Yes, Your Majesty."

"The whole affair is somewhat complicated by your, shall we say, unique gift?"

"What do you mean?"

"I mean, as someone with the gift of visions you are privy to information that we lesser mortals are not. Therefore it is difficult to know what you saw, versus what you might have...intuited."

"There's no way that girl was some sort of vision. I touched her. I promise you, she was real."

"In the end," King Henry continues as if I haven't said anything, "I decided upon the simplest course of action." He stands up, and I'm pretty sure this is the part where he's going to go all Henry VIII on me and either lop my head off or order one of his minions to do it. "I called your mother."

"*What?*" So not what I was expecting.

"I said, I called your mother. She was kind enough to give me her phone number when I visited your family's antique shop. I told her what occurred here tonight and asked her what conclusions she might draw from the episode—if it's possible that what you saw in the secret passageway is somehow a manifestation of your gift. I understand these kinds of things run in your family and I thought she might be able to shed some light on the situation."

"Awesome. I bet that was an enlightening conversation." My mom's gift is completely different from mine, and completely different from Gran's. And while Gran has chosen to share her gift with the world in the most obnoxious way possible, my mom has chosen the incognito route. No one except Gran and I, and my dad, know the specifics of her gift. And while she'd never fire me for having an involuntary blurting episode in her shop, I know she thinks there are things I could be doing to control my gift instead of arbitrarily spewing premonitions, or whatever the hell you want to call what I do. So I'm sure she loved getting a phone call from King Henry essentially asking her if I was as batshit crazy as the character I'm supposed to be portraying. Not to mention, she was at the airport, about to board a plane for Paris.

"Actually, she suggested I speak with your grandmother. Who is on her way here now."

I groan. "Super. That should be helpful." Not. "Why don't you just fire me and be done with it?"

"Mistress Verity, there may or may not be a dead body somewhere on my property. If there is, I need to find it. If what you saw was a vision of some sort, I would like to keep it from coming true. And I don't think firing you will help me accomplish either of those things."

There's a knock at the door, and Gran comes bursting in. She looks from me to King Henry and back again.

"So, you've got retrocognition now, too? Guess we should have seen that coming," she says to me. "No pun intended."

"Mistress Gilbert, thank you for joining us," King Henry says. "Please, have a seat."

Gran sits down and takes my hand. "The same thing happened to your Great Aunt Dorcas, you know. Of course, she wasn't always trying to avoid using her gift like you do, so she recognized the visions for what they were."

"This wasn't a vision, Gran. I swear—"

"Don't worry, kiddo, we'll work this out. In the meantime, I think you've given poor Mr. Bacon here quite the scare."

"Gran, I'm telling you, I didn't—"

"I assure you, Mr. Bacon—do you prefer Mr. Bacon or King Henry? Or perhaps Your Majesty? Was I supposed to curtsy? I'm not used to being in the presence of royalty. How about if I call you Hank? I feel like we're friends already, don't you?"

Hank is starting to get that glazed look he had in the antique shop when first confronted with my fruitcake family.

"Certainly, but could we—"

"You can call me Viv. Although I do like the sound of Mistress Gilbert. Anyway, Hank, I assure you that my granddaughter is perfectly sane and surely a wonderful addition to your staff here at Tudor Times. We've been encouraging her for years to seek out a mentor who could help her with her gifts. The addition of retrocognition to her psychic abilities could be the perfect impetus."

"Retrocognition? I'm not familiar with the term," King Henry says.

"In its simplest terms it means being able to see past events. Which is, I'm sure, what must have happened here tonight. You do know that Lunewood Castle is an authentic sixteenth-century castle brought over stone by stone from England? Of course you do. Well, there's no telling how many people died in this place over the centuries, and no doubt some of them met a rather unfortunate end."

I'm about to protest, but Gran squeezes my hand. Hard.

"Was the girl you saw wearing modern clothes, dear?" she asks me.

"No, but—"

"Well, there you go. It was obviously a flashback from the past."

"You are certain of this?" King Henry asks Gran.

"No one's been reported missing, have they? Juliet's vision was no doubt just a new facet of her psychic ability. One that I'm sure she'll master in no time and use to every advantage here in her position as the Psychic Maid, or whatever she's called. Won't you, dear?" She gives me the look that means do-exactly-what-I-say-or-pay-the-consequences-and-they-will-suck.

I nod.

King Henry considers us both for a long moment. "Well then, Mistress Verity, please let me know if there's anything I can do to help you, er, adjust. Perhaps Angelique has some tips she could share?"

"Sure," I say. "Good idea." Angelique should be really helpful. I'll get right on asking the fake psychic about my new fake psychic power.

"In the meantime, if you should have any more visions of dead bodies on the premises, I ask that you inform me immediately."

"Understood, Your Majesty."

Gran stands up and pulls me with her. "Thank you, Hank. You have a magnificent place here. I'm sure Juliet will greatly enjoy working at Tudor Times. So sorry to have worried you. We'll be on our way."

King Henry stands as well. "Good night, Mistress Gilbert. Thank you for...elucidating things." He gives us a little bow. "I'll expect you here at one o'clock tomorrow, Mistress Verity. And we'll try this again."

"Thank you, Your Majesty. See you tomorrow."

"Give my regards to Lady Anna. I hope my call did not distress her overmuch."

I hear Gran stifle a snort as she pulls open the study door. "I'm sure she's very grateful for your concern, Hank," she says, and I'm not sure which of us is the bigger liar.

Chapter Nine

Thanks for Throwing Me Under the Bus

"What the heck, Gran? Thanks for throwing me under the bus. I am so not ever going back there," I say as we make our way to the staff parking lot.

"Of course you are."

"No, I'm not."

"We'll discuss this in the van."

I unlock my bike and stow it in the back of the antique shop van.

"Can I drive?"

"No."

"Why not? The least you could do is let me drive after making me look like a total whack-job."

"Get in the van, Juliet."

I get in on the passenger side and Gran pulls out of the staff parking lot and onto the narrow, winding road leading down the hill from Lunewood Castle going all of fifteen miles per hour.

"Are you sure it's safe to ride your bike on this road? There's barely enough room for a car."

"Well, if I had my own car it wouldn't be a problem, would it? But since I'm never coming back here it doesn't matter anyway."

Gran sneaks a glance at me, then goes back to white-knuckling the steering wheel.

"I don't even *have* a Great Aunt Dorcas."

"I know, dear."

"Then why the hell did you make all that up about me having retrocognition? There's no way that dead girl was a hallucination. I touched her. She was real."

"I know she was, dear."

"What?"

"What you saw was real. That doesn't mean it wasn't a hallucination."

"That doesn't make any sense."

"Of course it does. You saw a dead girl. But whether she was a part of the physical world or a vision of the future remains to be seen."

"You really think I might have imagined her? That it's some new blip in my 'gift'?"

"Whether she's a blip or not, you saw her and that means something. For the time being I would prefer for Hank Bacon, and anyone he talks to, to think you're seeing things that aren't really there. Sometimes it's beneficial for people to think you're nuttier than a fruitcake, dear. And this is one of those times."

"How do you figure?"

"Hank told me you claimed the girl you saw had been strangled."

"Yeah. She had a thick gold chain wrapped around her neck. It was cutting into her skin."

"So, how do you think that chain got there? If what you saw wasn't a blip, as you call it, that means someone is responsible for strangling that girl and hiding her in a secret passageway. And I'm fairly certain they don't want anyone drawing attention to that fact or they wouldn't have bothered to hide her in the first place. But if the only person who claims to have seen the body happens to be nuttier than a fruitcake..."

"No one will take me seriously. Super."

"Which means you're not a threat. And therefore not worth strangling."

"It also means I'm never going to get asked out on a date. And forget prom. I might as well become an actual nun." I lean my head against the window, and we drive in silence for a while as I ponder my woeful future.

"I give up. Screw saving up to buy a car. I'll just ride my bike to school and have sweaty helmet hair for the entirety of my high school career. I am *not* going back to Tudor Times tomorrow and acting like I hallucinated a dead body. I'm enough of a freak show already. I'm sure it's perfectly fine when you're old and people can just call you eccentric, but when you're sixteen years old and have never been kissed and most of your peers already treat you like a pariah, being a psychic weirdo totally sucks."

"Juliet, honey—"

"I'm not done yet! Did you know the Maid of Kent is a nun? A nun! Nuns do not wear fabulous gowns that give them awesome cleavage. Also, Elizabeth Barton, that's the Maid of Kent's real name, was known as the *Mad* Maid of Kent because most people thought she was batshit crazy. How ironic is that?"

"On the contrary, dear. It sounds to me like you've found the perfect job."

"Why does the perfect job have to involve me behaving like a freak? And do you seriously want me to work someplace where someone is strangling people? I'm sure Mom will be delighted with the idea. Which reminds me, what's up with her telling Hank to call you?"

"She was about to board her flight. And you know how your mother is. She doesn't like discussing the family gifts with outsiders."

"I'm sorry I'm such an embarrassment to her. It must be nice to have a gift you can hide."

Gran pulls into our driveway and turns off the van. "Juliet, we all have our ways of coping. Your mother's gift is every bit as frustrating as your own. She spent years getting the credentials necessary to back up what she already knows just by touching something. Your mother can't explain why she can do what she does, but she's found a way to live with it and even use it to her advantage. You would do well to do the same. That's all your mother wants for you. How you cope is up to you, but I will tell you that hoping your gift will magically disappear is a waste of time. You will never be 'normal.' And the sooner you embrace that, the better off you'll be."

"Gee, that sounds super, Gran, but what am I actually supposed to *do*?"

"'I think that somehow, we learn who we really are and then live with that decision.' It could be worse, you know. Your Great Aunt Velva had that thing with rodents, and she never did figure out how to get rid of them."

"As if being named Velva wasn't bad enough. I should have been a boy. None of the men in our family are cursed, right?"

"To the best of my knowledge only the women bear special gifts. Unless you count Velva's brother Vester, who I understand had a peculiar talent for playing musical instruments with his nose."

"If you're trying to make me feel better, it's not working."

"'Remember always that you not only have the right to be an individual, you have an obligation to be one.'"

"Oh God. Please stop quoting Eleanor Roosevelt. I hate it when you do that."

"Fine. But you have to admit the woman was a genius. Now let's go inside and you can tell me all about Tudor Times. I expect Cami will be along any minute. She's worse than Gladys Kravitz."

"Who's Gladys Kravitz?"

"She's a nosy woman who lived next door to a witch. Never mind, it's from a television show before your time. You think your family is nuts? Just be glad you don't have a mother like Endora."

Gran heads inside and I've just finished putting my bike away when Cami's kitchen door flies open.

"You're back!"

"Yup."

"How was Tudor Times? Did you see Grayson? Did he admit he's madly in love with you?"

"Yes, I saw Grayson. And do you know what I was *wearing* when I saw him?"

"A sumptuous Tudor gown that gave you unbelievable cleavage?"

"No, that would be Bree Blair with the gown and the cleavage. Because she also works at Tudor Times."

"Seriously? Bummer."

"You have no idea. She gets to play one of Henry VIII's beautiful young wives. Guess who *I* get to play?"

"I thought you were supposed to be a psychic maiden or something."

"Yes, the Maid of Kent. Do you have any idea who the Maid of Kent was?"

"A psychic maiden?"

"Correct. She also happened to be a nun. A batshit crazy nun, I might add."

"Whoa. Double bummer." She winces and then obviously tries to rally. "But if she's crazy that totally takes the pressure off, right? You can blurt away with total abandon."

"Just don't. I could've happily gone the rest of my

life without finding out what a wimple is."

"What *is* a wimple?"

I give her a death glare and stomp into the house.

"So, no cleavage, huh?" she says, trailing me to the kitchen.

"If you'll excuse me," I say, throwing open the freezer door, "I don't have time to discuss my lack of cleavage and unattainable boys with fantastic abs. I have a double date with Ben and Jerry." I grab a container of New York Super Fudge Chunk and pry the lid off.

Cami gets out two spoons and throws me one. "Well, how did the psychic part go?"

"The psychic part was unexpectedly awesome. It was the dead body part that sucked."

Cami freezes with her spoon halfway to her mouth. "The *what*?"

"Yeah. It's a long story."

"Good thing I've got all night," Cami says, pulling up a chair.

Gran puts on a pot of tea, and Cami and I excavate fudge chunks while I give them both the lowdown on my first day at Tudor Times, including the part where I tried to hide from Grayson so he wouldn't see me in my nun costume. And then I tell them about how I found myself in a secret passageway looking down at a dead girl. Who promptly disappeared.

"What the hell?" Cami says.

"I know," I say. "And then King Henry called Gran and she came to Tudor Times and convinced him I was nuts."

"Why would she do that?" Cami asks, looking questioningly at Gran.

"Because if I'm just the crazy psychic girl no one will take me seriously," I explain.

"That sucks."

"Being strangled to death sucks more," Gran interjects.

"As of right now it's just my word that the dead girl even existed. And if no one believes me, I'm not a threat to whoever killed her and then made her disappear."

"You so have to go back and find out who she is and what happened to her. And you have to do it without getting murdered, okay?" Cami says.

"That shouldn't be a problem since I have no intention of ever going back."

"What? Why not?"

"Gee, lemme think. Why would I want to pass up dressing like a nun and acting like I'm nuts while working in a castle where someone likes to kill people and make them disappear? Yeah, it's a tough call."

"But Jules, what if whoever strangled that girl kills someone else? And you could have stopped them?"

"Seriously? That's what you're going with? You're not even going to ask me if I'm sure she was real and not just a hallucination?"

"Either way, you need to find her," Gran says.

"What's that supposed to mean?"

"It means you need to figure out if that girl was real or a 'blip,' as you so eloquently put it."

"So you're perfectly fine with me going to work someplace that potentially has a murderer on the loose?"

"That reminds me," Gran says. "I have something for you." She gets up from the table. "I'll be right back."

"So, does Grayson look good in tights?" Cami asks while we wait for Gran to return.

"I am so going to kill you. I had to wear a freaking nun costume. Do you have any idea how bad wimple hair is?"

"Again, I ask, what's a wimple?"

"It's a word that shouldn't even be in my vocabulary."

"But your Prince Charming came to the rescue, right? I told you he likes you."

"Cami, seriously, quit it with the whole Grayson-is-secretly-in-love-with-me thing. It's not funny."

"But I swear he likes you! He's always staring at you. He obviously—"

"He obviously has a girlfriend. And Bree Blair is the only thing standing between me and daily humiliation at the hands of the Josh Gaddises of Lunevale High. There's no way I'm getting on her bad side."

"Bree Blair doesn't *have* a bad side."

"Yeah, that's my point. I have *no chance* with Grayson. He and Bree are clearly totally into each other, they have all these inside jokes and are constantly together. I mean, have you seen the way he looks at her?"

"I saw the way he looked at her in seventh grade. But when's the last time you saw a PDA from those two? It's like they're an old married couple or something."

"Just because they're not swapping spit on the quad like Whitney Petty and her flavor of the month doesn't mean they're not in love. Some people prefer to keep that stuff private."

"So, if Grayson Chandler was your boyfriend, you wouldn't feel the need to make out with him every chance you got?"

I'm momentarily distracted by the image of Grayson and me making out in the middle of the quad. I blink it away. "Stop. Just stop it, Cami. It's not going to happen. Not for someone like me, with someone like Grayson. If he happens to be staring at me it's probably because he's waiting for me to have a PTS moment and do something embarrassing."

Cami shakes her head. "It's not like that. You sell yourself way too short, Jules."

"You're my best friend. You're obligated to say that."

"Here it is!" Gran comes back into the kitchen and hands me a small pink cylinder. It looks like a fat tube of lipstick with a loop of black cord attached to it.

"What's this?"

"Backup."

I pull the lid off the cylinder and instead of lipstick there's a small LED light and two tiny metal prongs. I press one of the two buttons at the base of the cylinder and the LED light comes on. "A flashlight? You're giving me a fancy faux lipstick flashlight to protect myself? Gee, thanks, Gran."

"Press the other button," Gran says.

I press the button. There's a loud crackling noise, and Cami tips over backward in her chair.

"Whoa!" she says, then stands up and rights her chair.

"She didn't even touch you with it," Gran protests.

"I know, but it caught me off guard. I have a very strong startle reflex. Don't ever try to sneak up on me. Just ask Jules."

"Yeah, her auto ninja skills kick in when she gets scared. And it doesn't take much."

"Don't make me roundhouse you again, Blurt."

"Can we focus?" I say and press the button again. "A stun gun? You're giving me a stun gun to take to work? Is that even legal?"

"It is if I give you a note that says you're allowed to carry it," Gran says.

"Unless they had stun guns in the Tudor era, I'm pretty sure the ban on twenty-first century technology applies to lipstick-sized stun gun/flashlight combos."

"That's what that little pocket in your nun habit is for," Gran says.

"How do you know about that pocket? And that's definitely not what it's for."

"No, but at the risk of sounding blasphemous, I'm guessing a stun gun would be a lot more useful than a Bible if you find yourself confronted with a murderer."

"I'm not going to find myself confronted with a murderer. I told you, I'm not going back."

"Well, if you change your mind, consider that little gizmo your knight in shining armor. But it's for close-quarter contact only. If you have the option, scream bloody murder and run like hell."

"Or I could just bring Cami to work with me. All I have to do is hit the stun gun button and she'll go into ninja mode."

"You are so asking for another bloody nose," Cami says.

Chapter Ten
The Butterfly Effect

That night I dream about the dead girl. Except in my dream she's alive. I'm standing in the secret passageway staring down at her when she sits up and smiles at me. "No one cares about polyester," she says, then the stone floor disappears beneath me and I'm falling. I wake with a jolt and the remains of a scream dying in my throat.

Gran comes in and sits down on my bed. She gently pushes my sweaty hair off my forehead and says, "Want to tell me about it?"

"It was the dead girl from the passageway. Except she was alive."

Gran doesn't say anything, just continues to stroke my hair.

"The girl I saw was dead, Gran. I'm sure of it."

"You don't have to try to convince me, Juliet."

"You still think I should go back to Tudor Times?"

"It's your decision. But I've always been a big believer in the notion that things happen for a reason, which means there's an important reason you found that girl. And if I were you, I'd want to know why."

"You're not worried about whoever killed her coming after me?"

"As of right now whoever killed her is getting away with it. There's no body. No proof. If he, or she, takes you out they'll have the police all over them."

"Gee, that's comforting." I sit up. "I don't get it, Gran."

"Get what?"

"I understand your gift. You help people find their soul mate, and that's super awesome and people are über-grateful for what you do. And Mom uses her gift to make a living and keep people from getting swindled and all that. But what good is my PTS? What's the point of having my gift if I can't prevent dead bodies from disappearing or, more importantly, keep someone from getting killed in the first place?"

"Juliet, there's no way you could have prevented that girl's death. You'd never even met her."

"I know, but if I had I probably would have told her something like, 'Beware the purple garden gnome!' or 'You're going to fart in yoga class!' The stuff I say is ridiculous. All it does is embarrass me or the person I yell it at. It's beyond pointless."

"I doubt very much that the things you say are pointless, Juliet. I like to think you have the gift of butterflies."

"What the hell does PTS have to do with butterflies?"

"I think the things you say work a bit like the butterfly effect. You know, a butterfly flaps its wings somewhere in the rain forest and it causes a tornado in Iowa?"

"You've totally lost me."

"You can't see the changes that come about because they're so small to begin with. I'll give you an example. When you were six years old you were sitting in the bathtub and all of a sudden you shouted at me, 'The weevils are going to ruin everything!' and started crying. After I put you to bed I got to thinking. And I went into the kitchen and opened the flour and sure enough, there were weevils in it. I would have never noticed the damn things without my reading glasses on. And it just so happened I'd promised to make my famous caramel cake for the engagement party of one of my clients the next day."

"So I saved some people from weevily cake? Woo-hoo."

Gran holds up a hand to silence me. "So I ended up going to the store to buy flour at nine o'clock at night and I ran into Charlene Plimpton in the produce section and we got to talking, and we must have stood there for half an hour shooting the breeze. Well, Charlene called me the next day to tell me the old oak tree in front of her place fell down that night and landed in her living room. She said if she hadn't run into me at the store she probably would have been sitting on her couch watching *Survivor* and the tree would have smashed her flatter than a flapjack. My point is, Juliet, your comments aren't pointless. But there's no way of knowing what might happen as a result of the things you say. It's fascinating, really."

"Why can't I just say, 'Don't be in your living room at nine fifteen or you'll get squashed by a tree'?"

"Would you really say that? I think you have Psychic Tourette's Syndrome, as Cami so indelicately puts it, because it *makes* you say the things you *need* to say. I've always wondered if you were more willing to pay attention to your gift, instead of trying to quash it, whether you'd have more control. Haven't you noticed that some of your premonitions are much more precise?"

"What do you mean?"

"Sometimes you're aware of what you're going to say before you say it, and you give very specific information. Like your prediction for Cami about the lead in *My Fair Lady*. I think it's very interesting, don't you?"

"I try really hard not to think about my PTS, actually. Except to wish I didn't say stuff that makes me feel like a freak."

"No one can make you feel like a freak without your permission, Juliet."

"Um, I'm pretty sure that's not quite how Eleanor Roosevelt put it. But nice try."

"'You wouldn't worry so much about what others think of you if you realized how seldom they do.'"

"Yeah, well, when they do think of me, they think

I'm a freak."

"Then you must 'do what you feel in your heart to be right—for you'll be criticized anyway.'"

"Would you *please* stop quoting Eleanor Roosevelt?"

"'You gain strength, courage, and confidence by every experience in which you really stop to look fear in the face. You are able to say to yourself, "I have lived through this horror. I can take the next thing that comes along." You must do the thing you think you cannot do.'"

"Whatever, Eleanor. I'm going back to sleep."

Gran gets up. "'A woman is like a tea bag; you never know how strong it is until it's in hot water!'" she calls as her parting shot.

Chapter Eleven

You Really Are Psychic!

’m eating breakfast the next morning and trying not to think about dead bodies or Tudor Times or the butterfly effect when Cami knocks on the kitchen door, then pokes her head in.

"Hey, Blurt. What's up?"

"Breakfast. Want some?" I gesture at the bacon and eggs Gran insisted on making for me before heading out in Rosie to run some errands.

"Yum," Cami says and goes to the cupboard to get a plate. "So, what time do you have to be at work?"

"I'm still not sure I'm going back."

"What do you mean? You have to go back! You have to find the dead girl."

"Yeah, that's what I was thinking—until I remembered that in order for there to be a dead girl, someone had to kill her."

"Are you sure it was a real live dead body? I mean, you know what I mean."

"Yeah, I'm pretty sure. I've never seen a dead person before, but she wasn't a mannequin or anything, if that's what you mean. And there's no way she was alive. Her eyes were all weird and she didn't blink once. And I was staring at her for a while before I fully processed what I was seeing."

"And then she was just gone? I mean, by the time King Henry went into the passageway?"

"I guess. I didn't follow him in there or anything, but he said there was no body, and it wasn't there when Grayson and I went back inside to check."

"You don't think King Henry could've hidden the body, do you? I mean—no body, no crime, right?"

"He definitely had enough time, but that would mean he was the one who strangled her, wouldn't it? Why else would he hide the body?"

"Someone had a reason."

"I know."

"You have to go back."

When I took the job at Tudor Times all I wanted was the chance to make some money, wear a fancy gown, and ogle gorgeous-but-taken Grayson Chandler from afar. The reality is so far from the scenario I imagined, it makes me want to cry. A disappearing dead body was definitely not part of the plan.

"You have to, Jules."

"I know."

"It really is the perfect job for you."

"Minus the nun habit and the dead body."

"Duh. So, what's your plan?"

"I thought I'd put on a deerstalker cap and an Inverness cape and walk around with a pipe in my mouth."

"That ought to be effective."

"I think the word you're looking for is 'elementary,' my dear Watson."

I'm feeling pretty good about my decision to return to Tudor Times and give the whole nun thing another shot, and then I talk to my mom. Not surprisingly, she's hideously jet-lagged after having spent her entire red-eye flight worrying about me instead of sleeping.

"I'm calling Hank," she tells me after I give her my version of the whole disappearing dead body thing.

"What? Why? What do you expect him to do?"

"Well, people are *dying* inside his castle, surely he ought to do *something*?"

"Don't worry, I'll be fine. Gran gave me a stun gun."

"Oh God. Please tell me you're joking."

"Nope. I'm all set."

"Juliet. I don't want you going back there. It's too dangerous."

"Oh, come on, Mom. It's the only job I haven't gotten fired from yet, and I'm pretty sure it's the only one I'll ever have where being a freak with a blurting disorder is considered a plus."

"Juliet Hope Verity, you are not a freak."

"I know, I know. No one can make me feel like a freak without my permission. Don't worry, nothing's going to happen to me. Everyone thinks I'm nuts, remember? Why would anyone want to kill me? I'm completely harmless. Unless your maple has tar spot and then, watch out!"

"The problem with that theory is that you're expecting a murderer to be rational. Let me talk to your grandmother."

I take the phone to Gran, who's in the middle of planting more pink begonias in the front yard. "It's Mom. Good luck," I say and escape to my room.

Gran knocks on my door half an hour later.

"How'd it go?" I ask, pulling off my headphones.

"The short version is, you can go to work today, but if anything happens to you, your mother will defenestrate me. Or maybe it was eviscerate? Anyway, she's calling Hank Bacon. The poor man."

"Great. As if he needs any more grief."

Gran smiles. "They're both doomed. Auras never lie." She winks and rubs her hands together like some nefarious cartoon villain.

"Yeesh. Creepy much?"

"Oh, and your mother also said to tell you she loves you very much."

"And to please not embarrass her any more than I already have?"

"Good golly, you really are psychic!" Gran says.

"Hardy har har."

Chapter Twelve

We Found a Clue!

"What the hell happened to you last night?" Angelique says when I report for duty in the Oratory. "You never came to the dining room, and rumor has it you had some kind of freak-out yesterday and Hank had to call the police."

"What? That's ridiculous!"

"Obviously. It's not like you'd be at work today if Hank had called the police on you, right?"

"Yeah, well, for the record, I did freak out, but there were no police involved, and I'm not supposed to talk about it."

"Why not?"

"It's complicated."

"Really? You're not going to tell me?" Angelique sits down at the small table and rubs the sides of her belly.

I try to imagine her strangling someone to death and can't, so I peek into the hallway, then close the door. "I'll make you a deal," I tell Angelique. "I'll tell you what happened if you help me figure out what it all means."

"Ooh, a mystery! I'm in."

"Last night, when I was on my way to the staff dining room, I accidentally triggered an opening to a secret passageway in the main hallway downstairs."

"You mean the one behind the suit of armor?"

My mouth falls open. "Yeah, how'd you know?"

"It's the only entrance in the main hallway."

"How do you know that? Hank didn't even know about it."

She shrugs like it's no big deal. "A couple of days ago I saw someone coming out of the entrance behind the suit of armor and decided to investigate."

"Seriously? What did they look like? Was it a girl? Did she have brown hair?"

"Whoa, sister. Why don't you finish telling me what happened last night. You triggered the secret entrance and then what?"

"And then I found a dead body in the passageway and freaked out."

Angelique's eyebrows disappear underneath her wimple. "For real?"

"For real."

"Who was it?"

"That's what I need you to help me with."

"Why? Didn't Hank know who it was?"

"That's the problem. By the time Hank got there, the body was gone."

"No shit? Where'd it go? Weren't you watching it?"

"No, I wasn't watching it! I wanted to get the hell out of the passageway. I'm not used to finding dead bodies. Plus, I think there was someone else in there with me. Someone alive."

"Whoa. Creepy. So what'd you do?"

"I figured out how to open the entrance again, and then Grayson, he's a guy from my high school who works here, and this knight named Drew were there, and Drew went to get Hank, and by the time Hank got there and checked out the passageway, the body was gone."

"Huh. What the hell?"

"I know. And then Hank called my grandma, and she convinced him that it was probably a vision of something that had happened in the castle years ago. And since no one's reported a missing person or anything, I'm pretty sure Hank has dismissed the whole thing as some sort of whacked-out hallucination."

"Have you ever had a hallucination like that before?"

"No. It wasn't a hallucination or a vision of the past or anything like that. She was real. And she was dead."

"What did she look like? Could you tell?"

"Yeah. She had brown hair, and her eyes were bloodshot and kind of clouded over but I think they were brown, too." I shudder, remembering her dead eyes staring up at me. "Her face was puffy, and she had this thick gold necklace wrapped around her throat that I think must have been used to strangle her. And I don't think she'd been dead very long because she wasn't, you know…"

"Putrid?" Angelique suggests.

"Yeah. That."

"What was she wearing?"

I try to picture the girl lying on the floor of the passageway. "She had white sleeves and a dark green or black bodice and skirt. Except for the white, her clothes sort of blended into the shadows. I really only paid attention to her face and the necklace."

"But she was wearing a costume?"

"Definitely."

"Brown hair, brown eyes. How old would you say she was?"

"Early twenties, maybe?"

"Hmm, I can think of like ten people that could be off the top of my head. What we need to do is find out who's missing."

"Hank didn't seem to think anyone was," I remind her.

"Well, just because no one knows she's missing yet, doesn't mean everyone is here and accounted for. We need to get a list of the people who work here."

"You think she was definitely a Tudor Times employee?"

"What else would she be doing in the secret passageway? Plus, you said she was wearing a costume. I'll ask around, see if anyone's noticed anything. In the meantime, let's check things out while we have the chance." Angelique gets up and heads for the door.

"Where are we going?" I ask as I follow her to the steep winding staircase that leads to the main floor.

"The dungeon."

"You're kidding, right?"

"I'm supposed to give you a tour of the castle, remember? Plus, the dungeon isn't open to the public, so we can go in there without anyone finding out."

"Why would we want to do that?"

"Just hush and follow me." She leads the way downstairs, past the main floor to a small basement storage room and then across a long hallway. "King Henry calls this floor the undercroft." Angelique points to various doors as we pass. "Those are mostly storage rooms. The dungeon is on the lower level of the Prison Tower, which is the one opposite the Rose Tower where we work." Angelique stops in front of a thick wooden door reinforced with iron bands. "This is it." She pushes up the heavy wooden bar on the outside of the door and leads the way into a dim room filled with strange-looking instruments. The only light comes from barred windows high up on the walls.

"No way. It's totally the Pit of Despair."

"The what?"

"Never mind. What's all this stuff doing in here?" I ask. There's a rusty iron cage hanging in one corner that looks big enough to hold an adult human, a chair with wicked-looking spikes on the seat and arms, a huge wooden frame set with rollers and ropes, and an entire wall hung with wood and iron instruments that look decidedly unfriendly.

"They're torture devices. Apparently the guy who built Lunewood Castle liked to collect them."

"Ew. This place is way creepy." I reach into my nun pocket to make sure my lipstick stun gun is there, in case I need backup. "What is that thing?" I point to a huge contraption in the corner that looks like an eight-foot tall statue of a young woman with a wooden head and a studded iron dress. One half of the woman's face appears to be rotting away, the wood obviously ancient and beginning to disintegrate. Her iron dress has a split down the middle with hinges on either side.

"That's the Virgin of Nuremberg, according to Floyd. You've met Floyd, haven't you? Old guy? Red uniform? Likes to refer to himself in the third person as the Keeper? His grandfather helped build Lunewood Castle, so he knows everything there is to know about the place. He claims it's a torture device from the fifteenth or sixteenth century. It originally had iron spikes on the inside that were designed to impale whoever was unlucky enough to get shut inside."

"Nice." I wrinkle my nose.

"Our King Henry doesn't seem to be into the torture scene. Or at least he's not into showing it off to the tourists."

"I can see why. I'd much rather eat a fancy dinner and watch hot guys sword-fight."

"Me, too. Okay, back to the dead body." She makes a beeline for a huge wooden cabinet on the far wall and opens one of the doors. "Check it out."

I walk over and look inside, expecting another gruesome torture device. The cabinet is empty.

Angelique reaches in and pushes something. The back panel slides open to reveal a dark space beyond. Angelique reaches into the front pocket of her habit and pulls out a flashlight. "I recommend you always carry a light. The wiring in this place is crap. Plus you never know when you might need to explore a secret passageway." She grins and gestures toward the darkness. "Shall we?"

"Oh, hell no."

"Come on, Jules, where's your sense of adventure? Don't you want to find out what happened to your girl?"

"I already checked the passageway yesterday. There wasn't anything in there."

"Yes, but you were looking for a body. We're looking for clues."

"What exactly do you think we're going to find?"

"I don't know. You can at least show me where you found the body."

"You do realize that if this was a movie you'd probably be the killer and I'd be a total moron for assuming you're innocent? Do you promise this isn't a ploy to lead me into the secret passageway so you can strangle me, too?"

Angelique makes the sign of the cross. "I promise. Besides, I would have killed you by now if I was going to."

"Thanks, that's so reassuring." Reluctantly, I pull out my lipstick stun gun and follow Angelique through the opening in the back of the cabinet and into the passageway. We walk a short distance until we reach a place where the passageway splits into two directions.

"The stairs to the main floor should be to the right," Angelique says.

"What's to the left?"

"I don't know. I haven't had a chance to check it out yet."

We go to the right, and Angelique leads the way up a twisted flight of stone steps.

"Okay, this is the ground floor," she says when we get to the top. She shines her flashlight down the passageway in front of us. "That bump in the wall is the back of the alcove in the main hallway where you found the entrance behind the suit of armor."

"How do you know all this?"

"I'm a snoop. I'm a fake psychic, remember? Being nosy is an occupational requirement."

Angelique starts walking slowly down the passageway with her flashlight trained on the dusty floor. We reach the bump in the wall and Angelique stops.

I look down at the empty space where the body was the night before. "It's not here," I say, even though that's patently obvious.

Angelique gets down on her hands and knees on the stone floor.

"What are you doing?"

"Looking for clues. You said there was no blood, right?"

"Right. I'm pretty sure she'd been strangled. So, no blood. Unless it's from my elbow. What exactly are you expecting to find?"

"I don't know. Do you see any scuff marks or anything that looks like someone might have dragged a body away from here?"

"You watch way too much *CSI*."

"Oh my God! Look!" Angelique shines her flashlight on the semicircular groove in the stone floor.

"What is it?"

"The chain around her neck, what did it look like?"

"Like one of those thick gold necklaces King Henry wears. The kind that goes across his chest? It was decorated with pearls and rubies or something. I'm not completely sure since it was kind of twisted and I was distracted by the dead girl whose neck it was wrapped around."

"Pearls?" Angelique says and pulls a pin out of her wimple.

"Uh, yeah. What are you—"

She sticks the pin into the crack at the base of the alcove and pries out a small white object.

"It's a pearl." She holds it out to me. "We found a clue!"

"You think it's from the necklace she was wearing?"

"What else would it be doing here?"

"What are we going to do with it? Should we give it to the police?" I ask, thrilled to have possible proof that the dead girl wasn't some sort of hallucination.

"Yeah, and we'll tell them my psychic powers led us to it."

I tuck the pearl into the pocket of my habit and help Angelique to her feet. "You don't think they'd believe us if we told them the truth?"

She shrugs. "We could try, but they'd probably just blow us off."

"Or?" I say. There's obviously an "or" coming.

"Or we could find the body and then they'd have to pay attention!" Angelique's eyes go wide. "Oh, wow. Oh my gosh, Jules."

"What? What is it? Do you know where the body is?"

She puts both hands on her belly. "No. I think my water just broke."

"*What?* Holy crap. What should I do?"

She takes a step toward me, then looks down at her feet.

"Shit, my sandals." She sticks out one very wet foot. "I paid a hundred and fifty bucks for these things."

I unpin my veil and hand it to her. "Here, use this."

"You're kidding, right? I haven't been able to reach my feet for weeks."

I kneel down and dab at her shoes with the wadded-up veil. "I think it's too late. They're pretty soaked."

"It's on my shift, too. Geoffrey's going to kill me." She takes a step back and looks down at the wet stone floor. "Shit, I contaminated the crime scene."

"I think we'd better get out of here. Can you make it down the stairs?"

"Yeah," she says, then winces. "Oh God. I think I'm having a contraction."

"Water stains are mightier than the sword!" I blurt as her face contorts with pain.

"Duly noted," she says once the contraction's past. "And if you figure out what the hell that means, let me know. In the meantime, I think I'd better get to the hospital sooner rather than later."

"Let's just go through the opening in the alcove."

Angelique points to her belly. "There's no way we'll both fit. And I don't know about you, but I'm so not staying in here by myself." She takes a deep breath. "Okay, I should have a few minutes before the next contraction. Let's go."

We head for the staircase leading to the dungeon.

"Are you okay going down the steps?"

"Yeah, but walk in front of me so you can break my fall." She grins. "Just kidding, I'll be fine."

We get to the bottom of the steps and make for the opening in the cabinet.

"Dammit!" Angelique stops in the middle of the dungeon.

"Are you having another contraction?" I ask,

trying to stifle visions of her popping out a baby on the dungeon floor.

"No, I'm pissed that I'm going to miss out on everything here. Okay, before we go back, here's the plan: first, you need to figure out who the dead girl is. She's got to be a Tudor Times employee. Check the staff sign-in sheet to see if anyone's absent. That should be a good place to start. Unless you want to have one of your psychic flashes and blurt out her name?"

"I wish. How am I going to know who's absent or what they look like? Are there any pictures of Tudor Times employees somewhere that I could look at?"

Angelique thinks for a minute. "Yes! Geoffrey has photos of everyone who wears a costume. He calls it his 'bible.' It's his record of who wears what and how their costume is supposed to look when it's put together properly."

"He didn't take *my* picture."

"He already has one of me. You should also try talking to Floyd. He's even nosier than I am, so he knows everything about everyone else's business. He lives in the gatehouse at the front of the castle and has been the caretaker here forever. He's also supposed to play King Henry's bodyguard, but mostly he creeps around spying on people. And he's a sucker for pretty young things, so don't be afraid to use your feminine wiles."

"Ew."

"Do you want do find the dead girl or not?"

"Well, yeah, and I'm flattered that you think

I have wiles, but in case you haven't noticed, I'm currently dressed as a nun."

"Oh, Lordy, here comes another one." Angelique puts her hands on the small of her back and bites her lip. After a minute or so she relaxes. "Okay, that ought to be enough ideas to get you started. Let's get out of here before I start crowning."

Instead of going back down the narrow hallway toward the Rose Tower, Angelique makes for a set of spiral stairs just outside the dungeon. "These will take us to the ground floor, down the hall from the Great Wardrobe. I need to get my clothes from my cubby. I'm so not going to the hospital dressed like a nun."

We make it to the ground floor landing and Angelique pushes open the door at the top of the stairs, then gives a yelp of surprise. I follow her through the door and find myself face to face with King Henry.

"Sister Elizabeth, is everything all right?" King Henry asks, and I can't tell if he's talking to me or Angelique.

"Sort of," Angelique says. "I was just giving the new sister here a tour of the castle and I'm afraid my water broke."

"Your water? Oh. Indeed. How may I be of assistance?" Somehow King Henry manages to look both flustered and disapproving.

"I need to get my clothes and my purse from the Great Wardrobe, and call my sister. She can take me to the— Oh, wow! Here comes another one!" Angelique grimaces and grabs my arm. "Your Majesty," she pants, "would you mind getting my stuff out of my cubby? I need my cell phone so I can call my sister. And I think we'd better hurry." She gives a low moan and King Henry takes off at a run for the Great Wardrobe, his royal robes flapping behind him. Angelique straightens up and lets go of my arm. "Okay, listen. This means you're on your own today, not just with the dead body thing, but as the Mad Maid of Kent," she tells me.

"Oh. Crap."

"Think you can handle it?"

"Sure. No problem," I say, but my nunly armpits are starting to feel uncomfortably clammy. At least black linen is good at disguising sweat circles.

"Be careful, Jules."

"I will. You faked that last contraction, didn't you?"

"Yup. I've got my phone right here." She pats the pocket at the front of her habit.

"Are you worried that King Henry's involved in all this?"

"No, I was trying to avoid Geoffrey. He's going to go nuts when he finds out I soiled my costume."

Chapter Thirteen

Keep Rocking That Fanny Pack

King Henry returns with Angelique's stuff, and she and I duck into one of the bathrooms where I help her back into her street clothes in between contractions.

"I shall escort you to the rear entrance," King Henry says when we come back out. He takes Angelique's arm and gives me a skeptical look. "Mistress Verity, are you prepared to take over as the Maid of Kent? We shall have guests arriving momentarily."

"She'll do great," Angelique says and puts a hand to her temple. "In fact, I'm having a vision of resounding success. *Pearls* of wisdom shall fall from her lips." She winks at me, and I remember the pearl in my nun pocket.

I reach my hand in to make sure it's still there and feel it nestled up against my lipstick stun gun. "Absolutely," I say.

"Tell Geoffrey I'm sorry about the costume." Angelique nods at the bundle of soiled nun stuff under my arm.

"I'm sure it's nothing a little soap and water can't fix," King Henry says at the same time I yell, "Fie, ignore the damned spot, I say!"

They both stare at me.

"Was that...?" Angelique asks.

"PTS? Yeah, sorry. Just call me Blurty McBlurterson." I hold up Angelique's crumpled nun costume. "I'll take this to Geoffrey. Good luck, Angelique."

"Thanks. Take care of yourself, Blurty," she says and gives me a hug.

"Let's get you to the hospital, Mistress Boden," King Henry says.

"Don't forget the bible," Angelique whispers, and then she and King Henry are off.

I'm hesitating outside the door of the Great Wardrobe when I hear a voice call my name. I turn to see Bree Blair coming toward me in all her queenly glory. "Oh my God, Jules." She pulls me into a tight hug. "Grayson told me what happened last night," she whispers. "You must have been so freaked out."

"You mean having to dress like a nun? Yeah, it's a bad habit." I'm really hoping this conversation isn't going where I think it's going, because the only thing that can possibly be worse than having to talk to Bree about Grayson is having to talk to Bree about looking for a disappearing dead body with Grayson.

"What? No. I'm talking about *the body*."

Yup, she went there. "Oh, that. Yeah, it pretty much sucked." So much for King Henry's orders not to tell anyone about the body.

She lets me go but continues the whispered conversation. "Are you sure it was real? It wasn't part of some sort of act King Henry was putting together?"

"In a secret passageway protected by a suit of armor? I kind of doubt it."

"How in the world did you end up in there anyway?"

"It's a long story."

"Miss Blair, if you're ready?"

Bree gives a startled hop, and we turn to see Geoffrey standing in the doorway to the Great Wardrobe.

"Oh, Geoffrey! You scared me, you silly!" She skips over to greet Geoffrey and they do this *très* French-looking thing where they kiss each other's cheeks multiple times.

"And how are you today, Miss Blair?" Geoffrey says as he puts a hand at the small of her back and steers her into the Great Wardrobe.

I follow in the wake of Bree's pristine crimson silk with my armload of soiled linen.

"I'm great," Bree says. "Where's Sarah? Did she finish fixing my pearl earrings?"

"Not yet. I have another pair you can wear for today."

Bree nods, then turns to me. "Geoffrey, you know Jules, right? Of course you do, she's the new Maid of Kent. Jules and I are classmates at Lunevale High."

"How nice," Geoffrey says. "Let's get your coif on, Miss Blair."

"I'm getting beheaded today," Bree tells me as Geoffrey busies himself with a complicated-looking headpiece.

"What?"

"It's part of a new Six Wives performance. We've been rehearsing it all week."

"Oh. Yikes. I thought you got to just stand there and look queenly," I say.

"I do. And then I get my head chopped off for sleeping around behind King Henry's back."

"Bummer."

"Truly."

I feel a little better knowing that at least I don't have to get beheaded. And then I make a mental note to check the Maid of Kent dossier to see how I die.

Bree fingers a luscious brocade fabric that's spread out on a long table in the middle of the room. "This is gorgeous, Geoffrey. What's it for?"

"A new doublet for King Henry. Wait until you see the trim."

"Oh, I bet it's yummy. He's so lucky to have you, Geoffrey. You're an absolute magician with fabric.

Jules, did you know King Henry stole Geoffrey away from Hollywood? He's even won an Oscar! Haven't you, Geoffrey?"

Geoffrey nods. "Yes, for *Little Minks*. It was my fourth nomination," he says demurely.

"Really? That's amazing," I say, looking at Geoffrey with new appreciation. "I love the dress Tibby Faye wore in the ballroom scene."

"Ah, yes. The blue gown. There were ten thousand Swarovski crystals on that dress. All hand-sewn," Geoffrey says and his eyes go all misty. "And the sequins! I was shedding them for weeks afterward. Even found them in my underwear. Not sure how they got in *there*."

Bree laughs. "Were you shedding feathers, too? That peacock dress in *Little Minks 2* was amazing. It must have taken forever to create," she says.

"I wouldn't know," Geoffrey responds. "I didn't design the sequel. The director decided to hire my assistant instead."

"Oh, were you working on another project?" Bree asks.

"No, I wasn't sleeping with the director," Geoffrey says.

There's an awkward silence and then Bree bursts out, "Ooh, how scandalous! And *unfair*! Is that why you let King Henry woo you away?"

"King Henry is a man with seemingly unlimited funds who understands the importance of craftsmanship and historical accuracy. How could I possibly pass up such an opportunity? The garments

I make for Tudor Times are not just costumes, they're re-creations, pieces of history you can hold in your hands, wear on your body. No one else can re-create history through fabric like I do. Did you know the British Museum has asked to borrow the costume I made for King Henry based on the Whitehall Mural? The British Museum!"

"I'm not surprised, Geoffrey. I've never seen costumes as beautiful as the ones here at Tudor Times," Bree says. "We're so lucky to get to wear them. Don't you think so too, Jules?"

"Uh, yeah," I say. "I've always wanted to be a flawlessly garbed nun."

Bree laughs. "Oh, come on, Jules. You somehow manage to look fantastic no matter what you're wearing. Me"—she gestures at her queenly ensemble—"I need the genius of someone like Geoffrey to make me look decent."

This is so not true it's ridiculous. I'm still trying to think of a comeback when Geoffrey finishes fiddling with her headpiece and says, "You're all set, Miss Blair. Your head will look quite lovely when they lop it off."

"I'm a little nervous. I've never been beheaded before."

"You'll be fine," Geoffrey says. "But don't get any fake blood on the costume or I'll have your head for real."

I look down at Angelique's sodden costume and cringe.

"I'll be careful, don't worry. Thanks, Geoffrey."

They do the cheek-kiss thing again. "Bye, Jules! Have fun today." And she's gone.

"Is something wrong with your costume, Mistress Verity?" Geoffrey asks me, eyeing my veil-less head and the wad of black linen in my hands.

"Sort of. Um, Angelique's water broke and I'm afraid some of it got on her dress and I tried to use my veil to dry her shoes off and, well"—I hold out the bundle of clothes—"they're kind of a mess."

Geoffrey looks at them, and I swear he gives an involuntary shiver of horror. "Put them in the laundry bin over there. I hope you didn't use Angelique's veil to mop the floor or something, because I don't have another one for you to wear."

"Oh, yeah. It should be okay." I sort through the bundle and pull out Angelique's veil. "It's a little rumpled but otherwise I think it's fine."

Geoffrey takes the veil from me like he's picking up a dirty Kleenex and doesn't want to get snot on his hand. "It will have to do. How in the world did you manage to get the rest of your costume so filthy?" He leans down and examines the hem of my dress.

"Oh, jeez, I'm really sorry. It must have gotten dirty when I was trying to help Angelique." In the dungeon. Or the secret passageway. Where clearly no one has dusted for decades.

"I can probably brush off most of the dirt, but you'll have to wait while I press the veil."

"Okay, thanks. I'm really sorry about the...water thing."

"At least it's not silk or it'd be ruined. And thank

goodness she had the decency to take her costume off before giving birth."

I'm trying to figure out if he's kidding or not when he wrinkles his nose at me and smiles.

"Did she get to the hospital okay?"

"She should be on her way there now. I wasn't really expecting to have to take over as the Maid of Kent so soon."

"I'm sure you'll do fine. I hear you've got the psychic part down at any rate."

"Oh?" I say, wondering what he's heard but afraid to ask. "I'm not really sure about that. It's more like I have this weird habit of blurting out random stuff that sometimes comes true."

"I see. How interesting," he says, but doesn't look the least bit interested.

I walk over to the rack of costumes, eager to change the subject. "These clothes are so amazing. How long does it take you to make one of these gowns?" I ask, realizing this could be the perfect opportunity to see if I can get Geoffrey to let me look at the costume bible Angelique mentioned.

"It varies. King Henry is a stickler for historical accuracy, which means no theater shortcuts with these costumes, so some of the more complicated pieces can take quite some time."

"How many have you made?"

"Oh, I've lost count by now. I've done at least three different ensembles for King Henry and one or two for each of his wives. And then there are all the knights and servants and other assorted characters."

"How do you keep track of it all?"

"Ah," he says, and smiles. "I've got my costume bible. It has photographs of all the ensembles and who wears what. Thank goodness for digital cameras these days. Makes it so much easier. Not like the days of the Polaroid."

"Wow, your bible thingy sounds awesome. Could I see it?"

"Certainly," he says, but he gives me kind of a funny look.

"That's a fantastic fanny pack, by the way. The black leather is very posh. And I love your costume. Did you make it, too? I'm just so fascinated with all the costumes you've created." I'm babbling but I can't seem to stop myself. What if I see a picture of the dead girl in the bible? What if I don't?

Geoffrey goes to one of the shelves and pulls out a large black binder.

"Be soft and attend thy soiled slops!" I blurt while his back is to me.

He turns and hands me the binder. "Here's the bible," he says, "and I assure you, my slops are quite clean, although I prefer the term 'trunk hose.'"

I have no idea how to respond to this so I say, "Of course. Thank you. Is it okay if I just..." I wave toward the stools tucked under one end of the table.

He nods, so I pull a stool out and open up the bible. I start flipping through the pictures, keenly aware that he's watching me out of the corner of his eye while he irons Angelique's veil.

"These costumes are so elaborate, " I say. "I can't

imagine how much it must cost to make one of these dresses."

"Money is no object for King Henry. And he insists that everything be exactly as it would have been in the sixteenth century."

"Does that mean the jewels are real, too?" I'm looking at a picture of a dress that looks absolutely encrusted with pearls, and thinking Hank Bacon must be a bazillionaire if they're real.

"Only for King Henry's personal garments and all except the diamonds. We use Swarovski crystals for those. Aside from the jewels, some of the fabrics cost over $200 a yard. A museum could never afford to commission that kind of reproduction, which is one of the reasons the British Museum has asked to borrow King Henry's Whitehall ensemble."

"That's amazing. I had no idea King Henry, uh, Mr. Bacon was that...dedicated." Translation: loaded.

On each page of the bible there's a picture of a Tudor Times staff member in costume followed by a detailed list of the costume pieces.

"Oh, hey! Trunk hose are pants!"

"Of course they are," Geoffrey responds.

"And a doublet is a jacket?"

"You're a quick study, Mistress Verity. Your veil is ready for you. I'll help you put it on if you promise not to need my services again until the end of your shift."

"Deal." I've reached the end of the book, and there's no sign of the disappearing dead girl. "And thanks so much for letting me look through your bible. You must be really proud of your work here."

"You could say it's the fulfillment of one of my greatest dreams." Geoffrey beams as he takes the book and puts it back on the shelf.

I hop down from the stool and stand still while he pins my veil into place, then brushes the dust off the hem of my habit.

"There you are, Sister Elizabeth. You're ready to channel the spirits, or whatever it is you do."

"Thanks, Geoffrey. You, uh, keep rocking that fanny pack." Ugh. Did I really just say that? I sound like a Bree wannabe. I cringe inwardly and flee the Great Wardrobe.

Chapter Fourteen
Don't Play Coy

I now know about trunk hose and doublets and have verified that everyone at Tudor Times has a way less embarrassing costume than I do, including the King's Fool and the guys who wear codpieces, but I'm no closer to proving I didn't hallucinate a dead girl.

I decide to head to the Rose Tower since I'm not sure what else to do. When I get to the Oratory I find a schedule for the day's readings already on the wooden table. I only have one private reading, but it's listed as a group reading, which is not something Angelique mentioned as a possibility. I feel a trickle of sweat slide out from beneath my wimple. I use the tent flap on my habit to wipe it away. All I have to do is act like a crazy nun. Should be easy peasy, right?

I prop open the Oratory door and prepare for the first tour group. According to Angelique, when I'm not doing private readings, and am just hanging out acting nunly while waiting for the next group of castle guests to come trooping through, I have a couple of options: I can kneel on the floor pillow and pretend to pray, or sit at the wooden table and pretend to write letters to supplicants, or I can study my Bible. Angelique suggested I bring a magazine to hide inside the Bible, which would allow me to look properly pious while secretly catching up on my celebrity gossip.

I decide to sit at the wooden table and write down what I know about the dead girl while pretending to write a prophetic letter to a sixteenth-century petitioner of the Holy Maid of Kent. I pick up a quill, dip it in the inkwell, and quickly discover that writing with a feather is easier said than done.

I've managed to scrawl, *Dead girl not pictured in Geoffrey's bible. What does this mean? And if she was murdered, who killed her and why???* when Floyd, aka the Keeper, knocks on the open door.

"There you are, Mistress Verity. I understand you're on your own today?"

"Yeah, Angelique's a bit busy having a baby."

"How convenient."

"Um, I'm pretty sure that's not how she'd describe it."

"I was referring to the fact that she's not available to answer any questions about all the excitement going on in the castle."

"Excitement?"

"Oh, come now, Mistress Verity. Or I suppose I should call you Sister Elizabeth? Either way, don't play coy with the Keeper." He gives me a wink and I suppress a shiver remembering Angelique's suggestion to flirt with him. He must be at least seventy-five years old.

"You've been snooping around where you don't belong."

"You mean the spirit world? I'm pretty sure that's my job."

Floyd gives a sinister-sounding chuckle. "I know everything that goes on around here, Mistress Verity. Everything. And I know you were in the secret passageway last night." He steps into the room and closes the door behind him. "How, may I ask, did you come to discover the entrance behind the suit of armor?"

"Oh, um, it was kind of an accident." Instead of feminine wiles, I'm now thinking about busting out my stun gun.

"I see. And who else was involved in this 'accident'?"

"You mean besides the sacrificial goat and the vestal virgins?"

Floyd is standing directly in front of the door, effectively blocking my only escape route. Unless I want to jump out a stained glass window.

"I *mean*, I would like to know who is sharing my secrets."

"Are you here for a reading? Because I don't have

you on the schedule." I hold up the handwritten sheet of paper with the day's readings. With my other hand I grasp the stun gun in my pocket and flip the lid off. "And I need to leave the door open if I'm not doing a private reading." I stand up and make a move toward the door, stun gun at the ready.

"Then tell the Keeper what you know, Sister Elizabeth." Floyd takes a step toward me and I jump back. He smiles, then pulls out a chair and takes a seat at the wooden table. "Do you truly have the gift of visions? Or are you a snooping charlatan like your predecessor?"

"Is there a third choice?"

"Come, Sister Elizabeth. I would hate to have to report you to His Majesty. He has far more important things to worry about than finding another Maid of Kent. In fact, I *insist* on a private reading. And since there is no one else here I don't see what's preventing you from fulfilling the Keeper's wishes."

"Perhaps if the Keeper weren't so creepy I'd feel more inclined to oblige," I say under my breath.

Floyd does his villainous chuckle thing again. "It's part of the Keeper's charm, is it not? The one-eyed bodyguard of a bloodthirsty king? The Keeper has to keep up appearances."

"The Keeper needs to make an appointment for a reading and Sister Elizabeth will be happy to oblige." I make a dash for the door and throw it open. And am ridiculously pleased to see a tour group coming my way. "Greetings, lords and ladies," I say loudly. "I have just finished a private consultation. Make way for the Keeper, if you please."

Floyd stands and pushes past me. "The Keeper hopes you find your time with the prophetess more illuminating than I," he tells the crowd, and disappears down the stairs.

The costumed guide leading the group, a young woman who plays another of Henry VIII's many wives, introduces me as the Holy Maid of Kent and explains my gift of prophesy.

"If we're lucky," she stage-whispers to the group, "she may have a premonition for one of us."

The group waits in hushed silence, and I take my time studying them. I hope they can't see the sweat that's starting to soak through my wimple. I spot a little girl in a pink T-shirt with a horse on it edging her way to the front of the crowd.

"Am I going to get a pet for my birthday?" she calls out. "I know I'm probably not going to get a pony, right?" She raises her eyebrows and looks at me with eyes full of hope. The crowd laughs.

I kneel down in front of the girl. "Greetings, fair maiden. What be thy name?"

"Hi. Uh, I be Maddy."

"Well met, Mistress Maddy. I am not at liberty to say whether or not you will get a pony of your own but I can tell you I see lots of pony rides in your future." This seems like a safe enough prediction.

"Awesome!" Maddy says and turns to the woman now standing behind her. "Hey, Mom! Can we do the stable tour next?"

"Sure, honey," the woman says, and smiles at me.

I give them a solemn nod, and the guide is gesturing for the group to move on when I feel a blurt coming on. "Pink toes make perfect pets!" I yell at Maddy, and then heave a sigh of relief that I've blurted something seemingly inoffensive.

Maddy cocks her head at me. "Pinktoes? Do you like tarantulas, too? Did you hear that, Mom? She said I should get a pinktoe tarantula!"

Her mom gives me an alarmed look, and I take back my sigh of relief.

"That's what you said, right?" Maddy asks me.

"Um." I pause, trying to figure out how to phrase my response. "The messages from the spirits can be very mysterious," I say. "My job is just to pass them on."

Maddy leans close and whispers, "Where are the spirits? Are they invisible? Do they like tarantulas, too? Pinktoes are the cutest. Terri Hoffer says I'm a weirdo because I like spiders, but Mom says everyone has their quirks. Do you have quirks?"

Ha! "Absolutely. Do you know what my Gran says?"

"Is she a spirit?"

I stifle a laugh. "Not yet. She says that you not only have the right to be an individual, you have an obligation to be one."

"Does your Gran like tarantulas?" Maddy asks, and her mom gives her hand a tug.

"I think our time's up, kiddo. Thank you, uh, Sister Elizabeth."

"Good day, milady. Thank you for visiting, Mistress

Maddy. I hope you enjoy the rest of your time at the castle."

"Bye," Maddy says. "Tell the spirits I said good-bye to them, too. I'm so excited for my tarantula! But I still wouldn't mind a pony."

"Duly noted," I say. "For now I think your stable tour will have to do."

Chapter Fifteen
You Are so Dead

I settle back down at my table, grateful to have survived both my encounter with the creepy Keeper and my first solo tour performance. A couple more tours go through and not only do I manage to avoid blurting out anything that might get me fired, no one looks at me like I'm some sort of freak when I bark out a completely random statement to a total stranger. They actually seem to like it. I'm starting to think this whole Tudor Times nun gig might be okay.

I just have to get through my private group reading and the dinner performance, and I'm home free. Oh, and somehow prove I didn't hallucinate a dead body. Without risking becoming the next disappearing dead girl. My group reading is due any moment, and I'm wondering if I'm going to bomb it, and then I think how handy it would be if I were legitimately psychic, because I would already know.

"Hey, Sister. Are you ready for us?" a voice calls from the doorway.

I look up and groan.

"What are you doing here?" I demand.

"I'm here to find out what my future holds," Cami says.

"And I'm here to make sure you're staying out of trouble," Gran says. "Do you have your Hot Lips on you?"

"My *what*?"

"Your stun gun. I hope you have it on you. I was going to sneak up on you and test your response time but Miss Stick-in-the-Mud over there wouldn't let me."

"Miss Stick-in-the-Mud doesn't like having to do CPR on little old ladies who sneak up on their stun gun–toting granddaughters," Cami retorts.

"Who you calling old, missy?"

"Don't worry, it's right here in my Bible pocket." I pat the front of my nun habit.

Cami snorts. "I can see why you hid from Grayson. You look like an extra from *The Sound of Music*." She starts singing, "How do you solve a problem like being a nu-un? How do you catch a knight and pin him down?"

"Shut. Up. What are you guys really doing here?"

"Can't your grandmother visit you at your place of employment without being suspect?"

"No. Especially not if you're plotting to jump me."

"Fine. I told your mother I'd check up on you. And I've been wanting to get a good look at the inside of Lunewood Castle for years. This place is the bomb-diggity."

"Oh, jeez. Please don't ever use that word again."

"I thought I'd see if they need a trumpeter or a Lady of the Bedchamber," Cami says.

"You're going to be way too busy rehearsing *My Fair Lady*," I say.

"Yeah, but that's not until August. Maybe there's another pregnant employee I could fill in for in the meantime?"

"Would you both please go away?"

"Not on your life, missy. I paid for a private reading," Gran says, "and I intend to get my money's worth."

"How's it going, anyway? Any more dead bodies?" Cami asks.

"No, but I think I found proof that the girl I saw was real."

"Really? What'd you find?"

I tell them about snooping around with Angelique and finding the pearl and then Angelique going into labor.

"Thank God you didn't have to deliver a baby in the dungeon," Cami says.

"Let's see that pearl," Gran says, and holds out her hand.

I give her the pearl, and she puts it in her mouth.

"Hey! What are you doing?" I demand. "That

could be valuable evidence."

"It may be evidence, but it's definitely not valuable," Gran says, and hands it back to me. "It's fake."

"Seriously?" I wipe the pearl off on my habit.

"It's too smooth."

"Do you think that's important?"

Gran shrugs. "She could have been strangled with a necklace containing fake pearls just as easily as real ones."

"Angelique suggested I look through Geoffrey's costume bible—it's this book that has pictures of all the costumed staff—to see if I recognized the dead girl, but I didn't see anyone who looked like her."

"You're sure she was wearing a costume?"

"Pretty sure."

"Can you find out if anyone's missing from work?"

"I can check the staff sign-in sheet. I guess I'll do that when I sign out tonight. But I don't know how to tell who's supposed to be here and who isn't. And since Angelique's gone, I'm stuck up here for the time being."

"Are you sure you're okay being up here all by yourself?" Cami says, looking around the Oratory.

"Yeah. I was a little freaked out when the Keeper cornered me in here but—"

"What? Who cornered you?" Gran demands.

"The Keeper. His name's Floyd Bean but he likes to refer to himself in the third person as the Keeper. He's a total creeper. He's King Henry's bodyguard-slash-castle-caretaker. Angelique told me to flirt with him to see if I can get him to give me some inside information because apparently he's all up in everyone's business, but"—I shudder—"that's so *not* going to happen. Besides the creep factor, he's like, seventy-something years old."

Gran clears her throat.

"No offense to seventy-something-year-olds in general. Hey, maybe you could have a go at Floyd?"

"He sounds like a real keeper," Gran says.

"Ha ha. Anyway, there are tour groups coming through all the time and I've also got the private readings, so I'm not really by myself much."

"Good. Maybe you should tell Hank Bacon about the pearl and let him do whatever he needs to do. No snooping around the castle by yourself, you hear me?"

"Yeah, I hear you. But he'll probably fire me if he finds out I was in the passageway again. I'd rather wait and see if I can figure out who the dead girl is first."

"You do what you think is right. But keep that stun gun at the ready. Now where's this young man you've got the hots for? I want to get a look at him."

"Number one, I am so not discussing my love life with you, and number two, don't you dare check out Grayson's aura."

"Well, how am I supposed to look at his aura if you won't show me who he is?"

"Exactly," I say.

"Have you seen him yet today? Did he say anything about the dead girl?" Cami asks.

"I haven't seen him, but he apparently told Bree about the whole dead body thing even though Hank told us not to."

"Can you blame him? That's some pretty juicy stuff."

"She asked me if I was sure the body was real. So Grayson no doubt thinks hallucinating dead bodies is another awesome skill in my freak-show repertoire."

"Well, then find the dead body and prove everyone wrong," Cami suggests.

"Yeah, I'll get right on that after dinner."

"When *is* dinner? I'm starving," Cami says.

"What time is it? There's a trumpeter guy who announces dinner at four. That's when I'm supposed to go to the minstrel gallery to spy on people."

"Ooh, I want to spy on people!" Cami says.

"You can't, you'll miss dinner."

"Can't we just spy for a little bit and then eat dinner?"

Gran looks at her watch. "It's three fifty-five. I'd say it's spy time."

They insist on seeing the minstrel gallery, and we all crowd onto the balcony to watch the proceedings in the Great Hall. Right on time the trumpeter plays the dinner announcement and the guests begin to flow into the hall.

"I'm supposed to pick out a victim to make a premonition about, and as soon as I've figured out who I'm going to target and what I'm going to say, I go downstairs and join the crowd," I explain.

"Okay, who should we choose?" Cami asks,

peering down at the castle guests.

"I've already got a great victim in mind," I say.

"Who?" Cami asks.

I wiggle my eyebrows at her.

"Me? What are you going to say?"

"I guess you'll have to wait and see. You'd better go find a seat."

"I think I'd rather stay up here," Gran says. "This is fascinating. It's like aura-watching at the mall only with a much better vantage point."

"Here comes the processional," I say as King Henry enters the Hall, followed by his retinue of lords and ladies and assorted hangers-on.

"Where's Grayson?" Cami asks.

"Yes, where is your young man?" Gran says, peering down at the procession.

"He's not my young man, he's her young man," I say, pointing at Bree Blair, who whispers something to one of her ladies-in-waiting before taking her seat at the head table.

"Oh, my," says Gran.

"I know," I say.

"How interesting," Gran continues. "I wonder if she knows?"

"Of course she doesn't know! I don't go around telling the girlfriends of the boys I'm in love with that I'm in love with their boyfriend. Not that she would care. She's like the most beautiful, perfect person ever. I'm absolutely no threat to her whatsoever."

"No, I don't think she'd see you as a threat," Gran says and snickers.

"Are you laughing at me?"

"No, but I am rather amused."

"How nice for you," I say, completely disgusted with her lack of loyalty. And then I realize she's giving me that weird squint she does when she's checking out someone's aura.

"Hey, stop it. What are you doing?" I wave my hands in front of her face.

"So very interesting," Gran says.

I cross my arms over my chest and turn my back on her. It's hard not to feel naked when Gran's doing her aura squint at you.

"That's him, isn't it?" Gran says and I turn to see her hanging over the edge of the balcony, full-on pointing at Grayson, who has just entered the Great Hall with Sir Drew. He's wearing his flowy white shirt with the green tunic that matches his eyes, and then he looks up and sees me and it's like someone zapped me with my own stun gun. I lose the warm and tingly feeling when I realize Gran is still pointing at him.

"Gran!" I hiss. "Stop pointing!"

She puts her arm down. "He's a hunk all right," she says, then looks back to Bree. "I wonder if *he* knows?"

"Knows what?" I demand. "What are you talking about? Nobody knows I like Grayson except Cami. And now you. Unfortunately."

Gran shakes her head. "It's not for me to reveal," she says.

"Damn right it's not," I say. "Jeez, Gran. I can't

take you anywhere. Would you please turn off your aura mojo and go enjoy your dinner?" And then a thought strikes me. "Wait a minute, how did you know that was Grayson? What does his aura look like? Does it match Bree's?"

"Oh, no you don't, Juliet. You can't have it both ways. Either you want me to keep my aura reading to myself or you don't."

"I don't, okay. I'm sorry, I just didn't want you to embarrass me. He totally saw you pointing."

"No need to apologize. I understand."

"So? What does his aura look like?"

She looks at me very thoughtfully. "I've learned that it's best to keep my meddling to people I'm not related to, or don't spend large amounts of time with."

"Oh, come on. You know you came here to look at his aura!"

"And, more importantly, to reassure myself that you're safe here."

"Whatever. You can tell me, Gran. I promise I won't freak out."

"Yes, you will."

"No, I won't! I promise."

"Juliet, the subject is closed. Whatever happens won't be because of my meddling."

"What's that supposed to mean? You *love* meddling! You're a matchmaker, for crying out loud. And what about your whole butterfly effect theory? You could be missing out on the perfect opportunity to flap your wings and cause a tornado!"

"I think I missed the tornado memo," Cami says.

Gran takes Cami's arm. "We'd better go, Mistress Cami. The dinner service is starting. Juliet, can you find out if the jester is single? He's a perfect match for a client I signed last week."

"Sure. As soon as you tell me if Grayson and I have matching auras."

"I won't tell you that. I will tell you that you should not take everything at face value. Look deeper if you want to know the truth."

"Let me guess, Eleanor Roosevelt?"

"Nope. Vivian Gilbert."

"You know what, Gran? *You* should take over as the Mad Maid of Kent. That's exactly the kind of crap I'm supposed to say to people."

"'Understanding is a two-way street,' Juliet. 'Friendship with oneself is all-important because without it one cannot be friends with anybody else.'" And before I can stop her she slips through the little door and I'm left alone on the balcony. I steal a few ogles at Grayson and then head downstairs to do my prophetic nun shtick.

When King Henry sees me enter the Hall he nods, and I give him a thumbs-up. And then I have to stop myself from running back out. Because now that I'm downstairs in the Great Hall instead of looking down at everyone from above, I'm realizing just how many people are going to be watching me. And one of them is Grayson. I'm fairly certain I now understand stage fright. I look over at Cami. She gives me a big wink, and I relax a little. At least I know I can count on her to totally ham it up when I make my faux prediction.

I rehearse in my head what I'm going to say and try not to steal glances at Grayson, who's sitting between two teenage tourists, totally oblivious to their admiring stares. He's watching Bree, who's talking to one of the other wives. I try squinting at Grayson, and then at Bree, to see if I can detect any trace of their auras. But all I can see is how ridiculously gorgeous they both are.

"Sister Elizabeth, have you had a vision concerning one of our guests? Sister Elizabeth?" King Henry's voice finally breaks through my pathetic preoccupation. I tear my eyes away from Bree's unblemished perfection. Everyone in the Hall is looking at me expectantly. Including Grayson. Oh God. Maybe I should just faint. The Maid of Kent was a big swooner, so it would be perfectly in keeping with my character. Except she usually passed out *after* she had her visions. I take a deep breath. "Your Majesty," I croak.

"Prithee speak up, Sister. Be not a blushet, thou art amongst friends here."

I clear my throat. "Forgive me, Your Majesty. But I have received a message from the spirits." I can do this. It can't be any worse than junior high theater camp, right? "I believe it concerns one of your guests."

"Indeed?" King Henry says, right on cue. "We are at your mercy, Sister. Please, tell us what you would have us hear."

I walk slowly over to where Cami and Gran are sitting. "I see a golden knight." I stop and stand in place like a statue with my hands in fists stacked at my waist. "He stands on a wheel with five spokes and he holds...a crusader's sword! He waits"—I pause to heighten the drama and then point at Cami—"for you."

She jumps out of her chair like a jack-in-the-box. "Oh, my gosh! A golden knight? Is it a statue? A golden statue?"

I nod. "You will meet this golden knight more than once."

"Oh my gosh! It's an Oscar, isn't it?" Cami flaps her hands around like she can't breathe. "Are you saying I'm going to win an Academy Award?"

"The honor repeats," I say, and then I wobble a bit for effect.

Cami grabs my arm. "Oh, thank you, Sister Elizabeth. You can't imagine what this means to me. I've been acting since I was five years old. I've always dreamed of winning an Oscar."

The room erupts in applause.

"Nice," Cami whispers in my ear. "If only it were a real premonition."

"Who says it's not?" I whisper back.

"Grayson looks amazing in that Prince Charming outfit."

"I know," I whisper back miserably. "And Bree looks like Cinderella post-bibbidi-bobbidi-boo."

The applause dies down and the crowd turns their attention back to King Henry.

"Ruination is found in a sequined gown!" I yell into the lull as King Henry opens his mouth to address the crowd.

Dead silence.

"Thanks, Sister Elizabeth," Cami says loudly and pats me on the back. "I'll make sure I wear something else when I accept my Oscar. A nun who gives fashion advice, who knew?" Cami totally mugs for the crowd as everyone bursts into laughter, and I take the opportunity to flee the Great Hall.

Chapter Sixteen

Tit for Tat

Floyd steps out of the shadows as I slip through the huge wooden doors propped open at the back of the Great Hall.

"Well, hello, Sister Elizabeth. We meet again," he says and tips his poufy red hat at me.

"And how is the Keeper?" I ask, feeling much less nervous in his presence knowing there's a huge crowd of people who can see us through the open doors if he decides to strangle me or something.

"Just keeping an eye on things, as is my duty. Too bad I only have the one." He taps his eye patch with a hoary fingernail. "I do hope I didn't frighten you earlier, Sister Elizabeth. I'm simply looking for a little tit for tat."

"Tit for what?" I feel a blush creeping beneath my

wimple.

"I'm suggesting a mutual exchange of information, nothing more, I assure you. I'd like to know how you came to be in the secret passageway, and seeing as how you've been snooping around the castle ever since you got here, I assume there's something you'd like to know as well. And given that my grandfather helped build the place and my family members have served as caretakers ever since, it's likely I have the answer you seek."

"So, if I tell you how I ended up in the secret passageway, you'll answer any question I ask?"

"Certainly. If I'm able."

I don't see what I have to lose, since I can tell him how I ended up in the passageway without mentioning anything about the dead body. "Deal," I say and I tell him about trying to hide in the alcove and accidentally triggering the opening behind the suit of armor.

"I see. So no one told you about the secret entrance?"

"Nope. Okay, my turn. Actually, I have two questions. Number one, who else knows about the passageways?"

He gives me a sly smile. "I can tell you that King Henry did *not* know about them. He was rather angry with me when he discovered their existence, thanks to you."

"You didn't tell King Henry about the passageways? Why not?"

"You never know when a secret might come in

handy." He gives me a wink. "I've told the King a few of Lunewood Castle's secrets, for his own safety you understand. Old Mr. Lune had quite a sense of humor. He used the passageways to play tricks on his houseguests, when he wasn't spying on them, that is. He also used them to pay special visits to some of his more attractive female guests." He winks at me again. "His granddaughter-in-law, the current Mrs. Lune, kept mostly to the ground floor and had everything else closed off to save on utilities. She never learned half the secrets my grandfather built into this place for old Mr. Lune. And now I'm the last living soul who knows them all. Mr. Bacon has been so focused on getting Tudor Times up and running, I hated to bother him with minutiae."

"I see. How thoughtful of you."

He gives me a wide grin, and his yellow teeth make me think of feral hamsters. "Prithee, tell me, what's your second question, Sister Elizabeth?"

The trumpeter starts playing the closing processional that signals the end of the banquet, and I turn to see King Henry and his entourage getting up from the high table.

"Is anyone missing today?" I ask Floyd.

"Missing?"

"Yes. Have you noticed if anyone is missing who should be here?"

"That is an interesting question. Who are you looking for?"

"Are you going to answer all of my questions with questions?"

"Perhaps. Does that bother you?"

"Dude. That's really annoying. Forget I asked."

"The Keeper will ponder your question and let you know when he has an answer."

"Great. Thanks. This has been fun. You're like a Tudor Magic 8 Ball. 'Reply hazy, prithee ask again.'"

"I should have thought a young woman with your talents would know the answers before she even asked the questions."

I give Floyd an eye roll and turn to go. I glance into the Great Hall and see Gran watching me. I give her a wave and make a beeline for the Great Wardrobe to change out of my costume. I am so ready to be done with Tudor Times for the night.

There's a small crowd of people in the Great Wardrobe who've also finished their shift. I grab my backpack and wait in line for an empty dressing room. When it's finally my turn, I change back into my street clothes and transfer my stun gun and the pearl to the front pocket of my capris. I give my hideous wimple hair one last look in the mirror and exit the dressing room.

"Jules!" Bree is standing at the front of the dressing room line, waiting to change out of her costume. She gives me one of her you-are-my-best-friend-in-the-whole-world hugs. "How was your first day flying solo? Did you hear Angelique had a baby boy?"

"No, I hadn't heard. That's awesome."

"King Henry was just telling me. He called the hospital before our dinner performance. I loved your premonition for Cami, by the way."

"Thanks. She's destined for stardom, our Cami." I smile at Bree and then look up to see Grayson watching us from the back of the line.

"It was perfect. The gown advice was my favorite part."

"Yeah, Tudor nuns are known for having their finger on the pulse of Hollywood fashion. Um, I'd better get going. I rode my bike and I want to try to beat the crowd down the hill."

"Oh, do you want a ride? I'm sure Grayson wouldn't mind. We should all carpool tomorrow so you don't have to ride your bike. That hill must be a killer."

"That's okay. It's fine on the way down, it's just that the road's really narrow, and now that I think about it, I can probably catch a ride with Gran and—"

"Hey, Grayson," Bree calls out, "we have room for Jules, don't we?"

Grayson walks toward us, and I subconsciously pat my wimple-hair.

"What's up?" Grayson asks Bree.

"Jules's bike will fit in the back of your car, won't it? It seems silly for her to have to ride all that way when we can easily take her home. Hang on, let me get out of this costume." Bree darts into an empty dressing room, and I'm left standing with Grayson.

"Hi," I say and attempt a dazzling smile so as

to distract him from my bad hair and any lingering aura of nunliness.

"Hi," he says. "How'd it go today? Better than yesterday, I hope."

"Uh, yeah. No dead bodies today, just the threat of imminent childbirth and a creepy guy with hamster teeth." I reach up to pluck a piece of straw out of his hair, and he inhales sharply as my hand brushes against his cheek. "Hay," I say, wanting to touch his cheek again. And his lips. And—

"Hey," he says quietly, his eyes locked on mine.

I swallow hard and hold up the piece of straw. "It was in your hair. Must be one of the hazards of being a squight."

He stares at the piece of straw and then looks toward the dressing room where Bree is making the transformation from Tudor queen to supermodel-worthy modern beauty. "Jules, I...I can't give you a ride," he says and walks away.

"I didn't want one anyway," I mumble, and throw the piece of straw in the garbage.

"I'm happy to see you made it through your shift without any more mishaps with your costume," Geoffrey says, eyeing me from his table in the middle of the room.

"Yup. It's a little sweaty but no afterbirth." I toss my costume in one of the laundry bins and feel a blurt coming on. "Sneaky cherubs lead the way!" I advise Geoffrey, which almost sounds like a normal thing to say.

He nods. "See you tomorrow, Mistress Verity.

Congratulations on surviving your first day as the Maid of Kent," he says, and I decide I could definitely get used to working at a place where people don't even blink when I let loose with one of my blurts.

"Thanks, Geoffrey. Keep rocking that fanny pack." I make a break for the exit, then stop dead in my tracks. Tacked up on a bulletin board next to the heavy wooden door of the Great Wardrobe is a hodgepodge of fabric scraps and snapshots of Tudor Times employees in costume. In one of the pictures there's a young woman standing next to Henry VIII. She's making some sort of adjustment to the heavy gold necklace lying on his chest while he grins directly at the camera. I recognize both the necklace and the girl. The last time I saw her she had it wrapped around her throat.

I've found the missing dead girl.

I grab one of the employees entering the Great Wardrobe. "Hey, can you tell me who that is?" I point to the snapshot.

"You haven't met Mr. Bacon?"

"No, not Mr. Bacon. The woman helping him with his costume."

"Oh, that's Sarah."

"Sarah?"

"Yeah, Sarah Buckley. She's the wardrobe assistant."

"Do you know if she's here today?"

"No clue. You could ask Geoffrey."

I walk over to Geoffrey's table and wait while he helps one of Henry's wives unpin her headdress.

"Did you need something, Mistress Verity?" he asks when he notices me hovering.

"I just wanted to ask you about your assistant, Sarah. Is she here today?"

"Sarah? No, she sent me a message last night that she had a family emergency and wouldn't be in today."

"Last night? What time?"

He sets the headdress down and puts his hands on his hips. "I don't believe I checked the time. You do ask a lot of questions, Mistress Verity. And here I thought you already knew all the answers, being psychic and all."

"I just...she looks like someone I saw the other night and I was wondering if it was the same person."

"Well, when she comes back you can ask her yourself."

"Yeah, okay. Thanks," I say, even though I know she won't be back. Ever.

Chapter Seventeen
Dying to Tell

I'm dying to tell someone I've figured out who the dead girl is. Okay, maybe that's not the best choice of words. I really, really want to tell someone I'm not crazy and I didn't hallucinate the girl in the passageway. I pull out my cell phone to see if I can catch Gran and Cami, and someone grabs my arm.

Certain that I'm about to get busted for using technology on the premises, I'm surprised when I look up into the worried face of one of King Henry's knights.

"Hey, I'm Mike. Can I talk to you for a minute?" Mike the Knight gestures for me to follow him a little ways down the hall. "You're the new nun, right?" he asks.

"Jules Verity," I say, holding out my hand.

"Mike Finkler. I play Sir Nicholas Carew, one of King Henry's Knights of the Garter. I heard you talking about Sarah."

"Oh." Crap.

"When did you see her? Was it last night?"

"Um, I'm not sure if it was her or not."

"Where was she? She was supposed to meet me after work last night and she never showed. I've tried calling her but she's not answering her phone."

Oh, jeez. I'm pretty sure Mike won't share my relief at discovering Sarah is my missing dead girl. "Geoffrey said she had a family emergency."

"Yeah, that's what he told me, too. Did you happen to notice if she was carrying anything with her? A jeweled weapon, like a dagger maybe?"

"Uh, no. I'm pretty sure she didn't have a dagger."

"Well, if you see her again, tell her I'm looking for her."

"Okay, sure." *You're not the only one.*

"Thanks. Good to meet you, Jules. I'll see you around."

dial Cami's number as I make my way toward the staff parking lot.

"Hey, where are you guys?" I ask when she picks up.

"We're halfway down the hill in Rosie. Are you off?"

"Gran brought the golf cart? I was hoping you guys could give me a ride."

"Your mom's van is a 'voracious gas guzzler' according to your grandmother. If you hurry, you can probably catch us on your bike."

I hear Gran say, "Ha ha," in the background. And then, "You'd better watch your carbon footprint, missy."

"Okay, I'll see you when I get home. I have news!"

"Really? What is it? Grayson Chandler *is* secretly in love with you? I knew it!"

"Oh, shut up. No. I figured out who the dead girl is."

"You did? That's awesome!"

"Yeah, except now I feel guilty about being relieved that she wasn't a vision of the past or whatever like Gran told King Henry."

"How'd you figure out who she was?"

I tell her about the picture on the wall in the Great Wardrobe and about my conversation with Mike the Knight.

"Are you going to tell Hank?"

"I haven't figured that out yet." I don't know what to think about Hank. On the one hand I can't really picture him having anything to do with murder. But on the other hand, it's his necklace, his castle, and his secret passageway—that he supposedly knew nothing about. "I want to see what I can find out about the dead girl first." And I want to find out if Hank is connected to her in any way other than employer and employee.

"Well, hurry up and get home. You'll probably beat us there. Ow! Your grandmother just punched me in the arm."

"You deserve it. Okay, I'm unlocking my bike right now. I'll see you in twenty."

"Ride safe."

"I will. Bye."

I strap my helmet on, hop on my bike, and head down the hill toward downtown Lunevale.

I'm pedaling along, thinking about Sarah, and the pearl, and wondering how it all connects, when I become aware of the sound of an engine behind me. The road leading up to the castle is narrow and bounded by hedges on either side so there not only isn't a bike lane, there isn't even a shoulder to scooch over onto. I slow down and inch over as far as I can, hoping the car will pass. Instead the engine sound gets louder and I turn to see who the dickhead is that's riding my ass. The next thing I know I'm flying through the air. I have time to think, *Well, shit,* before I hit the hedge and everything goes black.

When I open my eyes I'm pretty sure I've died and gone to heaven, because Grayson Chandler is looking down at me.

He cups my face in his hands. "Jules? Jules, are you okay? Please say something."

"You look really good in tights," I say.

He looks confused for a second and then laughs. "If I didn't suspect you have a head injury, I'd swear you were flirting with me, Juliet Verity." He lets go of my face and straightens up. "Are you all right? You were totally lights-out just now."

"I'm fine," I say. "And so are you." I smile at him dreamily.

"Uh, well, as much as I'd love to hang out by the side of the road with you, I think we'd better get you to a hospital."

"I don't like hospitals. They smell like misery and fish sticks."

"Jules, I think we should get you checked out," he says. "There's a huge crack in your helmet."

"Nah, I'm okay," I say and I knock on my helmet for effect. "Ow."

"I'm taking you to the ER. At the very least, you probably have a mild concussion."

Grayson pulls me upright and slings my arm around his shoulder. "Can you make it to my car?"

"Nope. You should probably carry me nestled in your arms. Oops, did I say that out loud? Ooh, look at the pretty stars. My head hurts."

Grayson pulls me against him and half carries me over to his car.

"This would be so much more romantic if you had a horse," I say.

He turns me toward him and leans down to look into my eyes. I'm about to pucker up when he says, "Your pupils look okay, but you're definitely dazed and confused."

"Yes, definitely," I say. "It's the head injury talking. A nun would never say such things."

He helps me into the passenger seat. "I'm going to grab your bike. Hang on a second."

I lean my head against the seat back and try to clear my muddled brain while he loads my crumpled bike, and then we're off.

"What happened?" he asks. "Did you hit a rock or something?"

"I don't think so." I play the scene over in my head. "I heard a car behind me and I looked back to see why they weren't passing and the next thing I know I'm lying on the ground looking up at you." I pause, remembering my tights comment. "Also, we should remember that I have a head injury and am not responsible for anything I might have said."

"Duly noted, although I kind of like Head Injury Jules. Not that I actually want you to have a head injury. So, yeah, I saw your bike on the side of the road and pulled over. You must have just crashed. What did the car look like?"

"I don't know. It happened so fast, I didn't really get a look at it."

"Are things always this dire with you?" he asks, and then he looks over at me and smiles and my insides go all melty again and I have to restrain myself from telling him that Head Injury Jules really wants to kiss him right now.

"It's been kind of a crazy couple of days," I say instead. *Do not think about how gorgeous he is. Think about the dead body. Or the fact that you are still wearing your bike helmet and probably look like a total doof. Do not think about the fact that you are alone in a car with Grayson Chandler and he is grinning at you like he's thrilled you're here. Focus on the fact that he has the sweetest, most perfect girlfriend in the world who has been nothing but kind to you even though almost everyone else at Lunevale High thinks you're a freak.* "Where's Bree?"

His smile disappears. "She got a ride home with Kaitlyn, her lady-in-waiting. She's kind of upset with me right now."

"Oh. I'm sorry."

"No, *I'm* sorry, Jules. If I had just given you a ride in the first place this wouldn't have happened. Do you think it was an accident? Just someone being a dick or did they try to run you off the road on purpose?"

"I don't know. Why would someone want to run me off the road?" And then I realize. The dead girl. I figured out who she is. What if someone was trying to shut me up? "The dead girl is Sarah Buckley, the wardrobe assistant," I say. I want someone else to know.

"The dead girl? You mean the one you saw in the passageway? Really? It was Sarah? How do you know?"

"I saw a picture of her in the Great Wardrobe. I'm sure it's her."

"You don't think it was a hallucination? Or some kind of, I don't know...psychic thing?"

"No. She was real. I don't hallucinate things. I mostly just have a blurting problem. Cami calls it Psychic Tourette's Syndrome because I can't control it. But it's really not a very accurate description because only like ten percent of people with Tourette's have a problem with blurting out inappropriate stuff, which is actually called coprolalia. But since I don't know what else to call what I do, her description sort of stuck." I'm babbling. I clamp my lips together and sneak a glance at Grayson.

He's staring straight ahead but his forehead is all crumpled up like he's struggling with a question on a calculus quiz. Or trying to figure out how to get me out of his car.

"Basically, I blurt out random stuff that usually makes no sense at the time, but is somehow important for me to say. At least, that's the current theory," I explain.

Grayson doesn't say anything for the next couple of miles and I wish I could take back my revelation. Coprolalia? Did I really need to go there? Maybe I should remind him again that I have a head injury.

He finally looks over at me and says, "So you didn't cheat on that math test in sixth grade?"

"Nope." I can't help but cringe when I remember how he looked at me that day. Like I was lower than the lowest lowly thing.

"Then how did you know the answers ahead of time?"

"I have no idea. And I only blurted out the answer to one of the questions so it's not like I knew all of them."

"You got suspended from school."

"I know."

"I'm sorry."

"You didn't know about my PTS. You thought you were turning in a cheater. The sad thing is, all

I wanted to do was ask you if you were interested in coming over to play Stormin' Da Castle."

"No way." He laughs and shakes his head.

"Way. I'd been dying to ask you ever since you came to school in your Anybody Want a Peanut? T-shirt."

"Wow, I had no idea you were a *Princess Bride* fan."

"Are you kidding? It's the greatest thing in the world. Except for a nice MLT."

"A mutton, lettuce, and tomato sandwich?"

"Yeah, where the mutton is nice and lean and the tomato is ripe. They're so perky, I love that." I pause. "I feel compelled to say that I'm just quoting Miracle Max here. I don't really like mutton. I actually think it tastes like wet wool."

"Inconceivable!" Grayson says. "I wish I'd known about our shared love."

I gulp and then realize he's still talking about the movie. "My dad took me to a special showing for the twentieth anniversary. I was instantly smitten."

"Me, too." Grayson gives me a dimpled smile and I remember how instantly smitten I was the first time I saw him looking like an eleven-year-old Westley in his Fezzik T-shirt. And then he got older and instead of noticing what was on his T-shirts I started noticing what was under them, namely his legendary abs. Of course, he was madly in love with Bree Blair by then and had been avoiding me for years on account of the whole math test disaster.

"I should have realized. You were the only person

who laughed when I read my *Morons* poem in Mrs. Keatley's class. I thought it was hilarious."

"It was hilarious. But you kind of had to know Vizzini."

"You're probably right. You have the best laugh ever, by the way." Grayson is quiet again and then he says, "What's a Hepplewhite, anyway?"

"What? Oh." Oh God, the booger blurt. "It's a style of furniture named after an English cabinetmaker."

"Furniture? Interesting. I'll let you know if I find any boogers. Although I have to admit, I'm not feeling very enthusiastic about the prospect."

"Yeah, no. I can't imagine how finding a booger depository is crucially important to your future. And somehow I don't think it's going to leave you madly impressed with my psychic skills."

"You can't..." He pauses. "I mean, you don't know how to read minds or anything, do you?"

I laugh. "Nope. My talent is completely uncontrollable, as far as I can tell. Sometimes I know what I'm going to say right before I say it, but usually I'm just as surprised as everyone else."

"Well, that's a relief. I can't have you going around reading my mind. That would be embarrassing."

"For both of us, I'm sure," I say and let out a hearty chuckle as if I find the idea amusing rather than terrifying. "You believe me about Sarah, right?"

"Of course. Why would you lie?"

"Did you know her? Sarah, I mean."

"Not really, but I think she was friends with Bree."

"Who isn't friends with Bree?" I ask before I can

stop myself.

"True," he says and glances over at me. "Did you tell Hank?"

"No, besides Gran and Cami, you're the only person I've told."

We pull into the ER parking lot. "Let's go get your head checked, Buttercup."

I barely manage to restrain myself from saying, "As you wish."

Chapter Eighteen

Someone's Got to Keep the New Nun Safe

We're the only ones in the ER, aside from an elderly man snoring in the corner. It's a quiet night in Candor County, apparently. A nurse checks me in while Grayson sits in the waiting room.

"What happened, honey?"

I tell her about my bike crash and show her my helmet. Grayson's right; there's a huge crack in it. I'm pretty sure my bike looks even worse. I have some ugly scratches on my arms and legs courtesy of the hedge, but otherwise I seem to be fairly unscathed.

"You're one lucky lady," the nurse tells me. "I'll have the doc check you over, make sure you don't have a concussion. You'll want to file a police report about the accident, okay?"

I say, "Okay," but I don't see the point. All I can tell the police is that I heard a car and then I crashed into a hedge.

The nurse leads me to a curtained-off space where a doctor shines a light in my eyes, asks me a bunch of questions, and tells me to take it easy for the next couple of days. And to get a new helmet.

"All right honey, you're free to go," the nurse tells me. "We'll let you get back to that cutie patootie in the waiting room. You're lucky in more ways than one, sugar." She gives me a nudge and raises an eyebrow.

"Yeah, uh, not really. But thanks."

"Hey, how'd it go?" Grayson asks.

"I guess I hit the hedge just right. I'm supposed to take it easy and come back in if I have any emergency symptoms of concussion, but otherwise I'm good to go."

We walk back to Grayson's SUV and he waits for me to put my seat belt on, then pulls out of the hospital parking lot.

"I called your grandma, by the way. While you were with the doctor. I didn't want your family to worry about you."

"You did? Wow. That was really nice of you. Also, brave. How'd you get her phone number?"

"Um, 1-800-ROMANCE? It's pretty hard to miss."

I groan. "Have I mentioned I come from a family

of freaks?"

"Yeah? Well, I bet you don't have a booger-encrusted Hepplewhite at your house. My money's on my little brother, by the way. He just turned five and he's a big nose picker. He also likes to do what he calls 'the nudie butt dance,' which involves running around the house with his underwear on his head. Bet you can't top that."

"I don't know, Gran does like to dance."

He laughs. "You live in the pink Victorian just off of Main Street, right?"

"Yup." The pink Victorian with the huge sign out front advertising An Aura of Romance. Just call 1-800-ROMANCE, that's my Gran.

We drive in silence for a bit, but it feels comfortable, and I realize with awe that I'm sitting in a car with Grayson without feeling nervous or embarrassed or panicked. "Thanks for taking me to the ER. And for calling Gran."

"Sure, it's the least I could do after putting you in harm's way."

"My crash so wasn't your fault."

"Yeah, well, I was still an ass for not giving you a ride."

"Consider yourself absolved of any assery."

"Thanks. I'm glad we had this chance to hang out a little bit. I feel so much better now that I know you're not a mind-reading cheater." He flashes his dimples at me, and now I'm a little nervous because I'm looking at his mouth and all I want to do is kiss it.

"Um, thanks?" I say instead of leaping across the

seat at him.

"Well, to be honest, I was more worried about the mind-reading than the cheating, but still. Color me relieved."

I so wish I could read his mind. Because part of me wonders... I give myself a little shake. *Get real, Jules.* Taylor Swift said it best, Bree's the cheer captain and I'm on the bleachers.

Grayson looks over and sees me staring at him. "Okay, now you're making me nervous. What are you doing?"

Oh, you know, dreaming about the day when you wake up and find that what you're looking for has been here the whole time. Except that aside from the cheer captain part, the girl in that song is nothing like Bree. "Just hanging out on the bleachers," I mumble.

"Uh, is that some sort of indecipherable psychic message?"

"No, but this is, 'My name is Inigo Montoya. You killed my father. Prepare to die!'"

"Faker."

"You're just lucky you don't have six fingers on your right hand."

Grayson laughs, and I don't want this moment to end. He looks so happy and being with him feels so...*inconceivable.*

"Are you working tomorrow? Or do you have to take it easy?" he asks when he finally stops laughing.

"I'll be there." *And so will Bree*, I remind myself, trying to quell the Taylor Swift video playing in my head. "I think I should talk to Hank about Sarah. And show him the clue Angelique found."

"Clue? What clue?"

I tell him about Angelique finding the pearl before going into labor.

"Wow. You don't do anything low-key, do you? Do you think the pearl was from the necklace you saw?"

"I think it has to be. Gran says it's fake. I don't know if that means anything or not. When Hank came into the shop"—I have a sudden inspiration—"wait a minute! Hank had on a heavy gold chain that my mom was drooling over when he came to our shop. It was the same kind of necklace Sarah was strangled with but a different design, and it was an actual piece of Tudor jewelry, instead of a reproduction. He was also wearing a fancy pendant that he'd commissioned. He was seriously pissed when Mom told him the jewels were fake. What if whoever sold him that pendant with the fake jewels, sold him the necklace Sarah was strangled with? That wouldn't make him mad enough to kill someone, would it?"

"I don't know. I can't imagine Hank strangling someone to death. But then, I can't imagine someone beheading their wives, either."

"Or murdering them to start a war with Guilder, like Prince Humperdinck. You just never know, do you? Hey, what do you think of Floyd?"

"Floyd? You mean 'the Keeper'? He's a character."

"He gives me the willies."

"Bree, too. And she likes everyone."

"You don't think he could be a murderer, do you?"

"To quote my favorite swordsman, 'Probably he means no harm.'"

"'He's really very short on charm,'" I quote back automatically.

"'Oh, you've a great gift for rhyme.'"

"'Yes, some of the time.'"

"You do realize it's a veritable tragedy that our eleven-year-old selves never got to hang out, right?"

"Yeah, but we probably would've grown up to be total cosplay nerds."

"Said the nun to the squight. Speaking of Tudor Times, let's get back to Floyd. I guess he could be a murderer, but he's no spring chicken. I kind of doubt he'd have the strength to take out a young, healthy twenty-something like Sarah."

"Okay, but he's still creepy. And he's a self-proclaimed hoarder of secrets."

"Yeah, Bree definitely thinks he's creepy, but she still flirts with him to get the inside scoop on everyone he spies on."

"Ugh. I think I'd rather remain ignorant."

Grayson pulls up in front of my house. "Here we are, Buttercup. Want a ride tomorrow? I can pick you up on my way to Bree's."

"Um…" I'm torn between wanting to steal every moment I can with Grayson, even though he's completely unavailable, and not wanting to torture myself by being the kind of girl who desperately covets someone else's boyfriend.

He hops out of the car without waiting for an

answer and pulls my bike out of the back. When I take it from him he puts his hands in his pockets and looks down at my bent front wheel. "Listen, Jules. Aside from the fact that your bike is trashed, I don't think you should risk riding to or from work by yourself. I think you need to be very careful until we figure out what happened to Sarah Buckley. I'll pick you up at twelve thirty, okay?" I can't quite read the expression on his face when he adds, "I insist."

"Are you volunteering to be my knight in shining armor?" I want to die as soon as the words are out of my mouth.

He looks me in the eye, then reaches out and brushes a strand of hair out of my face. "Someone's got to keep the new nun safe. Look what happened to Angelique." He grins. "See you at twelve thirty, Buttercup."

"Okay," I say, against my better judgment. "See you tomorrow." My face feels super hot as I wheel my bike up the walk. I turn back and Grayson gives me a wave. "Thank you, Sir Squight!" I call.

He waits until I reach the front door before pulling away.

Chapter Nineteen

You Can See That in Someone's Aura?

The front door flies open and Cami barrels into me.

"Jules, oh my gosh, are you okay?" She throws her arms around me and squeezes me tight.

"Ow."

She lets go immediately. "What is it? Are you injured?"

"No, you were squeezing me too hard. Help me put my bike away, would you?"

"Dude. I think you need a new bike."

"I know. Just open the garage door, okay?"

We put my bike away and then join Gran in the kitchen. She gives me a gentle hug but doesn't let go for a long moment.

"You can drive the shop van to work. Screw

the greenhouse emissions," she says. "And I'll run interference with your mom."

"That's okay. Grayson offered to give me a ride."

"Did he? He's a very thoughtful young man, your Grayson."

"He's not *my* Grayson."

"What happened?" Cami asks. "Tell us everything."

I tell them about the bike crash and my trip to the emergency room.

"Do you think it was an accident?" Gran asks.

"I don't know. That road is pretty narrow, and I'm sure there are plenty of lousy teenage drivers working at Tudor Times. It could have been someone who wasn't paying attention, was messing with their phone, or their stereo, or whatever.

"Did Grayson see anything?"

"No. He must have gotten there right after it happened. He said he saw my bike on the side of the road and stopped."

"Should we call the police?" Cami asks. "If someone pushed you off the road that's hit-and-run."

"Yeah, except I didn't see the car. I can't tell the police anything other than what I just told you. Which isn't much."

"We still need to report it, Juliet," Gran says.

"Okay, fine. But it's not like they can do anything about it."

"What if this is related to the body you found? And the killer is trying to keep you from talking?" Cami suggests.

"Yeah, that's what I was thinking, except, keep

me from talking about what? No one seems to be taking me seriously about having found a dead body. Wouldn't the killer be making things worse for themselves by running me off the road and possibly drawing police attention to Tudor Times?"

"Not if you're dead," Cami says.

"That's a nice thought," I say.

"Who could have overheard you asking about the missing girl?" Gran asks.

"The Great Wardrobe was full of people turning in their costumes. And there was that whole conversation with Mike the Knight. He seemed kind of nervous, but why would he bother asking me about Sarah if he was planning to run me off the road?"

"Who were you talking to outside the Great Hall while Cami and I were at the banquet?"

"Oh, that was Floyd. The Keeper. He's the one who cornered me in the Oratory. He wanted me to tell him how I found the secret passageway."

"You should stay away from that one, Juliet. His aura is a mess."

"How so?"

Gran shakes her head. "Some people's auras make me feel happy to be alive. His is like the cloud of stench surrounding a rotting piece of meat."

"Gross."

"And possibly dangerous. Do not let him catch you alone again."

"How about Hank Bacon's aura? Do you think he could have anything to do with the missing girl?" Cami asks.

"Whoever killed Sarah knew about the secret passageway, and according to Floyd, he never told Hank about it," I say.

"Yeah, but you and Angelique both found the secret entrance. Hank could have found one, too," Cami points out.

"True. And he was in the passageway by himself after I found the dead girl. He definitely had time to hide the body."

"I can't see Hank Bacon as a killer. It's not in his aura," Gran says.

"You can see that in someone's aura?" Cami asks.

"Well, no. But he's a perfect match for Anna and I know she'd never strangle someone in cold blood. So, unless I'm losing it in my old age, I don't think you have anything to fear from Hank. But somebody is certainly up to no good."

"Oh my gosh! I forgot to tell you my epiphany. Remember that necklace Hank was wearing when he came into the shop? The one Mom was all gaga over? Well, the necklace Sarah was strangled with was really similar, only it was decorated with pearls and rubies. What if whoever sold him the pendant Mom told him had fake jewels in it, sold him the jeweled necklace, too? Do you think that would make him mad enough to kill someone?"

"So he just strangles the nearest employee and drags her into the secret passageway?" Cami says. "Uh, yeah. I don't think so."

"Well, what if she was in on it somehow?"

"I think you should talk to Hank Bacon tomorrow,"

Gran says. "Show him the pearl and tell him you think the girl you saw was Sarah."

"Good plan," Cami says. "And now that that's settled, tell us about your knight in shining armor and how he came to your rescue again."

"He didn't come to my rescue, he drove me to the emergency room. And I think that was only because he felt guilty for dissing me in the Great Wardrobe." I tell them about Bree offering me a ride in his car without asking him.

"Ooh, do you think they had a fight about it?" Cami asks, and she and Gran look at each other.

I shrug. "I don't know."

"But you said he's picking you up tomorrow, right?"

"Yeah. On his way to Bree's house."

*G*rayson reappears promptly at twelve thirty the next day.

"Hey, Buttercup," he says as I hop into the passenger seat, and any chance I had of resisting his charms today floats away like the last flower petal in a game of she loves me, she loves me not.

"Hey, there," I say, while my brain screams "She loves you!"

"Got any predictions for me today?"

"Yes. Today you will escort a nun and a queen to a castle on a hill." And the nun will gaze at you adoringly the whole way.

He laughs. "Wow. I never would have seen that coming. You're good."

"I know. It's a gift."

"Speaking of gifts, you were right about the boogers."

"I was?" Awesome. I will forever be associated with boogers in Grayson's mind.

"Yeah, the Hepplewhite turned out to be a love seat my mom inherited from my great-great-grandmother. Apparently Ronan, my little brother, has been making deposits on the back of it for months, possibly years. My mom is furious. She's afraid it'll ruin the fancy silk upholstery fabric if she tries to clean the boogers off."

"I bet my mom could help. Tell your mom to bring it to the antique shop in August when she gets back in town."

"You sure your mom wants to be involved in a booger removal?"

I stifle a giggle picturing Mom's face when she sees the love seat. I wonder if her artifact dating ability applies to boogers? "I'm sure she's dealt with worse. Not from me, of course. I don't even have boogers."

"Me, either. How are you feeling, by the way? Any symptoms of concussion?"

"Nope. I feel kind of sore and a little scratched up, but otherwise I'm fine."

"Glad to hear it. No life-and-death drama today, okay?"

"Let's hope not. Hey, I Googled Sarah Buckley

this morning," I say. "Did you know she had an online costume shop?"

"I'm not surprised. I know she was into Ren Faire stuff."

"Ren Faire?"

"Renaissance Faire. You know, people dressed up in costumes walking around gnawing on turkey legs? Sarah's in the same guild as one of the knights at Tudor Times." Grayson looks over at me. "Hey, we should ask him if he knows where Sarah is!"

"Let me guess, Mike the Knight?"

"Are you doing that psychic thing again?"

"No, I talked to Mike yesterday. He heard me talking about Sarah and wanted to know if I'd seen her."

"Oh. Well, so much for that lead."

"Gran thinks I should talk to Hank and tell him about the pearl, and that Sarah is the girl I saw in the passageway."

"It can't hurt, right?"

"Well, he could fire me for sneaking around the secret passageways after he told me not to."

"Maybe you should blurt out, 'You will not fire me!' right before you tell him about the pearl?"

"Ha ha," I say, and Grayson grins at me and I forget to breathe until I notice we've pulled up in front of Bree's house. She comes bouncing down her front steps as I open the passenger door so I can climb into the backseat to let her sit in front with Grayson.

"Oh, no worries, Jules. I'll sit in back," she says,

leaning in to give me a quick hug. "Are you okay? Grayson told me about your bike crash."

"I'm fine. I just got a little up close and personal with a hedge. I don't really recommend it."

"I wouldn't think so," she says, then slides into the seat behind me. She leans between the front seats and gives Grayson a quick kiss on the cheek. "Hi, Gray. Off to work we go! Jules, I want to hear all about your psychic job. I'm absolutely fascinated by the gift of visions thing. Do you, like, communicate with spirits or how does it work? Will you do a reading for me?"

"Um, the reading thing is still kind of new to me," I say. "Angelique was teaching me her method before she had to go to the hospital, but mostly I act pious and nunly and blurt out random information at various intervals. Which, oddly enough, seems to entertain people instead of making them think I'm a freak."

"Why would anyone think you were a freak?"

"I'm fairly certain most of Lunevale High, not to mention the *town* of Lunevale, thinks I'm a freak thanks to the whole blurting thing."

"I don't think so, Jules. I think some people have a hard time dealing with things they don't understand, but you know what? The people who matter don't mind and the people who mind don't matter. Anyway, I've never thought you were a freak. I assumed you had a special gift like your grandma. She helped my aunt find her one true love. They got married last summer. It was so romantic."

"Really? That's awesome." Who knew? "Yeah, she's got a knack for romance, that Gran."

"I'm so jealous. Your family is so cool."

Whoa. Bree Blair did not just say that *she's* jealous of *me.* I would trade my "gift" for her supermodel hair alone. Not to mention her boyfriend. A girl can dream, right?

When we get to the castle Grayson leaves for the practice field to work on his knightly skills, Bree heads to the costume shop to pick up her "uniform," and I go in search of King Henry.

I knock on the door to his study and King Henry pokes his head out.

"Ah, Mistress Verity. The very lady I need. Prithee, do come in." He opens the door barely wide enough to let me through and that's when I see the two police officers sitting on his leather couch.

Chapter Twenty
The Police Are Summoned

*H*ank gestures at a chair across from the officers and takes a seat behind his desk. He's in his full-on Henry VIII regalia and he looks very stern and regal and like he might behead anyone who gives him any shit.

"Mistress Verity, allow me to introduce Officer Kilbride and Officer Lasky."

"Nice to meet you," I say, and the officers each give me a brief nod.

"Gentlemen, this is Juliet Verity. She's the young woman who claims to have seen the body in the passageway." He turns back to me. "Mistress Verity, I believe we've discovered the identity of the young woman you saw in the passageway."

"You have?"

"Yes. Yesterday, Geoffrey came to me with some very distressing news. He said he'd recently discovered that his assistant, Miss Sarah Buckley, had been helping herself to certain costuming materials—fabrics, trims, and most distressingly, the jewels used to decorate my garments. He believes she had been at it for some time and may have even been 'borrowing' some of my privately commissioned jewelry and weaponry in order to replace the valuable jewels with worthless fakes before returning the pieces to my personal inventory. We believe she must have had an accomplice. Geoffrey tells us that you were asking about Sarah yesterday—"

"Excuse me, Mr. Bacon," Officer Kilbride interrupts. "Would you mind if I asked Miss Verity a few questions before you go any further?"

"By all means," Hank says, and Officer Kilbride continues.

"Miss Verity, we really appreciate your help with this matter. Can you tell me, how did you come to be employed here at Tudor Times?"

"I saw an ad in the local newspaper and came for an interview. King Henry, I mean, Mr. Bacon, offered me the job on a trial basis and asked if I could start right away."

"I see. Do you have a previous relationship with any of the employees here?"

"Um, I go to high school with two of the employees, Grayson Chandler and Bree Blair, and there are a few others. I haven't met everyone who works here yet."

"Friday was your first day of employment?"

"Yes."

"And Mr. Bacon tells us you claim to have seen a dead body in a secret passageway off the Main Hall on Friday evening. Is that correct?"

"Yes. I was just coming here to tell Mr. Bacon that I'd figured out who I saw in the passageway."

"Indeed? Why don't you start from the beginning, Miss Verity, and tell us what happened Friday night."

"Okay, um, I was heading downstairs from the Oratory—that's where I hang out as the Maid of Kent—and I had just entered the main hallway when I heard voices coming from farther down and I, uh...I decided to hide."

"Why did you decide to hide, Miss Verity? Did you feel you were in danger for some reason?"

"No, I, um, just didn't want anyone to see me right then. So I ducked into this little alcove that contains a suit of armor and I was trying to squeeze behind the suit when my elbow bumped the ax that sits in one of the armored gloves, which triggered some sort of secret mechanism and then there I was in the passageway."

"And what did you see in the passageway?"

"Well, at first I couldn't see anything, and then I felt around and found a wall sconce and that's when I tripped over something on the ground that turned out to be a dead body."

"How do you know it was a dead body?"

"I didn't realize she was dead at first. She was lying on the floor staring up at me, and I was still freaked out by the whole revolving suit of armor thing and was kind of distracted."

"And what made you think she was dead?"

"Well, I basically fell right on top of her and she didn't react, and then I noticed she wasn't blinking and her eyes were all bulgy and weird-looking and there was this huge gold chain wrapped around her neck that was biting into her skin."

"I see. And did you recognize this dead girl?"

"No. Like I said, Friday was my first day of work here so I don't know very many people yet."

"And what is your job, Miss Verity?"

"I play the Maid of Kent. She was a Tudor prophetess."

"I see. And do you consider yourself a prophetess, Miss Verity?"

"Not really, no."

"Not really?"

"No. I don't consider myself a prophetess," I say, so of course my PTS decides this is the perfect time to prove my lack of prophetic skills. "Be alert to the squirt and smell the ketchup!" I yell and decide I should so get Eleanor Roosevelt bonus points for being an individual for that one.

Officer Kilbride's expression doesn't change, but he pulls a notebook out of his breast pocket and writes something down. When he's finished he looks up at me and says, "Miss Verity, I understand you're in the care of your grandmother, Mrs. Vivian Gilbert, who runs a matchmaking service in Lunevale?"

"Yes, that's my Gran," I say, knowing that any credibility I might've had left has been wiped out by

An Aura of Romance. And then I feel a surge of hope that maybe instead of thinking she's a total kook, he'll turn out to be one of Gran's satisfied customers, like Bree's aunt.

"And do you also believe that you can see auras?"

Rats. "No, sir. That's Gran's gift, not mine."

"And what is your 'gift,' Miss Verity?"

I totally set myself up for that one. "It's really more like a curse. I have this, um...blurting disorder thing."

"Blurting disorder?"

"Yeah. I'm not really sure what the purpose is, other than to humiliate me on a daily basis, but Gran thinks... Have you ever heard of the butterfly effect?"

"Yes, I have."

"It's kind of hard to explain, but according to Gran's theory, the smell of ketchup is the butterfly that might help you avoid a tornado."

"I see." He obviously doesn't.

"It makes more sense when Gran explains it. And the stuff I say almost never makes sense at first, but eventually turns out to be true somehow."

"So, you're saying that you *are* psychic?"

"I don't really know what I am, Officer Kilbride. But if you could let me know about the ketchup that might help."

"Did you want to make any other predictions while you're at it?" he asks. "Something about mustard, perhaps? Or maybe mayonnaise?" He smiles like we're condiment coconspirators.

"It doesn't really work that way." This is so not

going well. "I just sort of blurt stuff out at inopportune moments. Especially when I'm nervous or under stress."

"I see. What are you nervous about, Miss Verity?"

"I didn't say I was nervous." Why would I be nervous? Just because I'm being grilled by the police about a possible murder and at any moment I could blurt something that sounds way more suspicious than ketchup? Nah. I'm totally zen.

"You said, 'nervous or under stress,' did you not?"

"I said *especially*. And yeah, I find stumbling over a dead body stressful. Not to mention having said dead body then disappear. And having everyone think I'm crazy. And not knowing what I'm going to say when I blurt stuff out. I'm actually pretty relieved that I blurted something about condiments, if you want to know the truth."

I swear I hear Officer Lasky snicker, but when I look over at him he's staring intently at his own notebook.

Officer Kilbride clears his throat. "Perhaps we could get back on track here, Miss Verity?"

"Absolutely, Officer. I'm happy to oblige." Okay, what's the worst-case scenario here? The fact that they don't seem to believe me about the body means they can't possibly think I killed anyone, right?

"If you could describe the body you saw?"

"Sure." I force myself to focus on the facts. "It was a young woman, probably in her early twenties, and she had dark hair and dark eyes. I'm pretty sure she was wearing a costume. I remember seeing white sleeves and a black or dark-colored bodice, and she had a thick gold necklace wrapped around her neck. Like, digging-into-her-skin-choking-her, wrapped around her neck."

"Could you describe this necklace?"

"It was a heavy gold chain with squares about an inch and a half wide and it was studded with pearls and rubies."

"Is this the necklace you saw, Miss Verity?" Officer Kilbride holds up a photograph of a heavy gold necklace studded with pearls and red and black stones.

"Yes, I think so. It was kind of twisted when I saw it, but it looked very similar." I give Hank a penitent glance. "And I know I wasn't supposed to, but I went back into the passageway with Angelique and she found this." I pull out the pearl and offer it to Officer Kilbride. "Gran says it's fake."

Officer Kilbride takes the pearl, then looks at Hank and they have a moment of silent inscrutable communication.

"Also, I'm pretty sure the dead girl was Sarah Buckley. That's why I was asking about her yesterday. I recognized her in one of the pictures on the wall in the Great Wardrobe."

"That sounds quite reasonable. Thank you, Mistress Verity," Hank says. "You've been most enlightening." The way he says it, the word "enlightening" sounds more like "infuriating."

"Are you going to tell me what's going on? Did you find Sarah's body?" *I* don't feel the least bit enlightened.

"We do not currently know the whereabouts of Sarah Buckley," Officer Lasky butts in. "I have a couple of questions for you, too, Miss Verity, if you don't mind." He flips through his notebook. "I understand your mother owns an antique shop in Lunevale?"

"Yes, Love at Second Sight. But what does that—"

"And do you work there, Miss Verity?"

"Yes, when my mom's there. But she's doing some appraisal work in Europe at the moment." Which is where I wish I was at the moment.

"So, she's out of town?"

"Yes." I refrain from saying that Europe is *clearly* not in Lunevale.

"And when did she leave?"

"On Friday. Why are you asking me about my mom?" Oh God. What if they call my mom?

"I'd like to run a little scenario by you, Miss Verity. Would you indulge me for a moment?" He says this like I have the option to refuse.

"Um, sure?"

"In this scenario you are helping Sarah Buckley remove the jewels from Mr. Bacon's Tudor replicas and then replace them with fakes. When Mr. Bacon comes into your family's antique shop and your mom tells him the jewels in his pendant are fake, you realize the gig is up and you and Sarah formulate a plan. You take the job at Tudor Times so you can help Sarah stage her disappearance."

"That's some scenario," I say. I can't tell if he's

being serious or just messing with me for some reason. I look at Officer Kilbride, but he's busy flipping through his notebook. "And there just happened to be a job opening at Tudor Times right when I needed one?" I ask Officer Lasky.

"As I understand it, Mr. Bacon recently discovered that one of his employees was pregnant. Would you happen to know how he came by that information or would you like me to enlighten you, Miss Verity?" He continues without waiting for a response. "Now, where was I? Oh, yes. You take the job so that you can be the one to find Sarah's body, which, conveniently enough, disappears before anyone else sees it. So Miss Buckley escapes with the jewels while we fruitlessly scour the castle for her body."

"Does that mean you've actually looked for her?"

"I assume Miss Buckley gave you a cut of the jewels which you plan to sell using your mother's connections?"

"Her 'connections'? Are you serious? My mom runs an antique shop, not a jewel-smuggling ring. Pardon me for saying so, but your 'scenario' is ridiculous," I say in a carefully controlled tone instead of yelling, "Are you a freaking moron?"

"As is the smell of ketchup causing a tornado," Officer Lasky says.

Touché.

"I believe we're done here," Officer Lasky announces and both officers stand.

"FYI," I say, "I know you probably won't believe me because I have no proof, but someone ran me off the road on my way home from Tudor Times last night. I don't know if it was an accident or someone trying to hurt me on purpose, but I thought you might want to know."

Hank looks alarmed. Officer Kilbride looks mildly interested. And Officer Lasky has obviously checked out already.

"Did you file a police report, Miss Verity?" Officer Kilbride asks.

"No, I was going to do that today. And here you are, so I'm reporting it."

"Do you have a description of the car?" Officer Kilbride asks.

"No, it happened too fast and I blacked out when I landed. Another Tudor Times employee saw my bike and stopped to help me. He took me to the ER."

"Mistress Verity, the next time something like this happens, and I fervently hope there will not be a next time, please notify me immediately," Hank says. "I will not tolerate reckless driving on my property, and if it was indeed a hit-and-run it should have been reported without delay."

"Well, hopefully it *was* an accident, because if there is a next time I might be too dead to report it."

"I would hate to see that happen, Miss Verity," Officer Kilbride says. He reaches into his shirt pocket and pulls out a card. "I strongly suggest you call me when you're ready to tell me whatever it is you're trying to hide." He follows Officer Lasky to the door and turns back one last time. "We'll be in touch, Mr. Bacon."

Chapter Twenty-One

Am I in Trouble?

"There's no way they actually think I have some kind of jewelry forgery scam going, right?" I ask Hank once the officers are gone. "Because that's ridiculous."

"I would agree, Mistress Verity."

"But I really did see a dead body."

"I believe you, Mistress Verity. Our interactions thus far lead me to believe you are truthful to a fault."

"Somehow I don't think you mean that as a compliment. Your Majesty—Mr. Bacon—I hope you know there's no way I'd make something like this up. It would obviously be pretty bad for your business if people heard you had dead bodies lying around the place."

"Indeed it would. But if there *is* a dead body, and

if someone purposely drove you off the road last night, then seeing that justice is served matters a great deal more to me than my bottom line."

"Did the police even look for Sarah's body?"

"I showed them the secret passageway and told them where you said you saw the body."

"Thanks for believing me. I promise I won't go back in the passageway. I have no desire to try to catch a murderer or anything. I just wanted to prove that I'm not crazy and I really did see a dead girl."

"Are you certain she was murdered?" Hank asks.

"Well, I guess she could have choked herself with your necklace, but it seems like a pretty ineffective way of killing yourself."

"How do you know she wasn't pretending to be dead?"

"Unless she used to work as a statue or has been taking lessons from old Mr. Farley, aka the Corpse, she was definitely dead. I'd much rather she was alive, but I don't think that's a possibility."

"We shall see."

I can't quite figure Hank out. With his Henry VIII obsession I feel like there should be a sense of fruitcake solidarity between us; at the same time I have to wonder if a person with that level of obsession can be completely credible. Which is what makes me say, "Can I ask you a question?"

"Certainly, Mistress Verity."

"Did you really not know about the secret passageways? Before I found Sarah, I mean?"

"I've been rather distracted with preparing for

the opening of Tudor Times. I'm afraid I've neglected a few things I shouldn't have. After we closed last night I went through the secret entranceway in the alcove and conducted a thorough exploration."

"No sign of a dead body, huh?"

Hank shakes his head.

"I hate to ask but, how much do you trust Floyd? He said he knew about the passageways and didn't tell you."

"I think Floyd makes a better friend than an enemy, Mistress Verity. And as he knows all of Lunewood Castle's secrets, I would have thought he'd do a much better job of getting away with murder had he committed one. If that is indeed what we're dealing with and not some elaborate jewel forgery scam as the police seem to believe."

"You don't really think I'm in cahoots with Sarah Buckley, do you?"

"I think Officer Lasky thought there was something you were holding back and was trying to get you to confess whatever it was by making preposterous suggestions. At least I hope that's the case."

"I swear I don't have anything to confess. I've told you everything I know. I even told you I went back into the passageway after you told me not to."

"You said you were trying to hide behind the suit of armor. Why? You weren't in some kind of danger, I hope? If you were, you must tell me."

"The only danger I was in was being seen in a nun outfit by the guy I've had a crush on since sixth grade."

Hank guffaws. Seriously, there's no other word for his laugh. "Well, now. It's all starting to make sense," he says.

"Yeah, except for the part where the body disappeared."

"Yes." Hank is instantly serious. "That part is truly vexing. One set of stairs in the passageway leads down into the dungeon and the other up into my private chamber." He makes a steeple with his pointer fingers and taps them together. "How long would you say it was between the time you exited the passageway and I entered it?"

"I don't know, maybe five to ten minutes?"

"Curious. I wonder if... Never mind." He waves a hand in the air in dismissal. "This is a discussion for the police. I do not want you involved in this any more than you already are. Someone knows the truth of what you saw in the passageway and that someone is, according to you, potentially a murderer. I intend to post a squire outside the Oratory for your safety today. I do not want you going anywhere in the castle alone, is that understood?"

"Yes, sir."

"Then may I suggest I escort you to the Great Wardrobe to get your costume and then perhaps you could enjoy a quick meal in the staff dining room while I see about finding you a squire?"

"Lead on, Your Majesty."

*W*hen we get to the Great Wardrobe there's no sign of Geoffrey, which is a relief since I can't help but feel like he was trying to implicate me somehow in Sarah's jewel forgery scheme.

I change into my nun habit while King Henry waits in the hallway bellowing "Greetings, fine sir!" and "Well met, madam!" at passersby. When I'm properly nunned out he leads the way to the staff dining room, which is tucked into the northwest corner of the castle.

"Enjoy, Mistress Verity. I shall send a squire to take you up to the Oratory." King Henry bows and takes his leave.

I go over to a long wooden table loaded with an enormous amount of food that looks pretty much like what they serve the castle guests. There are baskets piled with huge slices of bread, plates of cheese, chafing dishes filled with roast beef, salmon, sausages, chicken, artichokes, turnips, carrots and peas, and at the far end, a selection of puddings, fruit and custard tarts, and the cute little marzipan animals.

I load up a plate and find a seat at a corner table. There are a few people scattered around the room in various stages of Tudor dress, and anyone who's eating is wearing some sort of smock over their costume.

"You're not supposed to eat in costume unless you're part of the banquet in the Great Hall, but you can just throw one of these on." A guy dressed in a white-and-blue tunic and tights grabs a folded square of fabric from a stack near the door and hands it to me. Then he pulls out the seat across from me and sits down. "So, you're the new nun, eh?" He grabs one of the carrots off my plate and pops it into his mouth. "I'm Jared. Squire to the great and noble Sir Henry Courtenay, Earl of Devon and Marquess of Exeter. Which basically means I clean up horse shit all day."

"Jules Verity. Crazy psychic nun."

"Good to meet you, Jules. I hear you found a dead body."

I blink at him for a second and then say, "Well, that's a relief. And here I thought I'd hallucinated it."

"Word is it was Sarah, the wardrobe assistant. So, how'd they do her in? Was there lots of blood?" He reaches for another carrot, and I resist the urge to slap his hand.

"I take it you weren't friends with Sarah?" I say, pulling my plate closer to me.

He chews on his carrot. My carrot. "I don't think anyone here was friends with Sarah. If being a bitch is grounds for murder there are plenty of suspects at Tudor Times. In fact I've got plenty of motive myself."

"Um, are you sure you should be telling people that?"

"I said I have motive, I didn't say I killed her. Why would I be asking you about her if I did her in myself?"

"Because you're...crazier than the Mad Maid of Kent?"

"Nah, I'm not crazy. Just insanely handsome."

He gives me a leering grin, and I manage to stifle the urge to gag.

"I hear Sarah was stealing stuff from King Henry," he continues.

"Where'd you hear that?"

"Word gets around." He leans forward. "Get this. Apparently, Friday night she sent Geoffrey a text saying that she had some sort of family emergency, but it turns out she didn't."

"She didn't?"

"Well, obviously the killer sent the text since she was clearly lying dead somewhere in the castle. Which is where it gets truly sinister."

"It does?"

"Yeah, I heard the police checked her cell phone records and guess where she was when she supposedly sent that text message?"

"Where?"

"Somewhere. Inside. The castle."

"Seriously?" I don't know what any of this means, but the feeling of dread I'd managed to stifle after finding Sarah's body is now working overtime.

"Seriously. And then it's like she just disappeared." He splays his hands out. "Poof."

"Tell me about it. How do you know all this stuff, anyway?" If what he's saying is true, I can't help wondering why the police didn't bother sharing it with me.

"My girlfriend's mom works in dispatch for the Lunevale Police Department. And you know what else?"

"What?" I lean forward in my chair.

"The guy who built this place, Mr. Lune, was apparently a total whack-job. Like, he built a bunch of secret rooms and an underground torture chamber and stuff. What if Sarah's still alive and she's trapped in the underground torture chamber?"

I lean back. Sarah is most definitely *not* still alive. "Then why wouldn't she just call someone on her cell phone?"

Jared looks disappointed. "Oh, yeah. Good point. Listen, babe. I've got to get back to the steeds. You going to eat that last carrot?"

"Yes. I am," I say, curling my arm protectively around my plate.

"You know," Jared says, looking at me thoughtfully, "you're pretty hot for a nun."

"Ew. Just take the carrot." I push the plate toward him. "I've lost my appetite."

"Thanks, babe." He grabs the carrot, gives me a wink, and takes off.

Chapter Twenty-Two
I'm the Crazy One

I'm picking at my roast beef, waiting for my court-appointed squire, when I get the neck-tingling feeling that someone is watching me. I look up to see Floyd leaning in the doorway to the dining room.

He tips his hat at me and ambles over. "Sister Elizabeth, I believe you've been holding out on the Keeper." He wags a finger in my face.

"Oh?" I say, leaning as far away from him as possible. After Gran's description of his aura I can't help picturing a stinky black cloud following him around.

"When you asked the Keeper about the secret passageway you somehow failed to mention the dead body."

I'm not sure how to respond. I decide to go for

naive innocence. "I know. And I'm really sorry. But I couldn't say anything because Mr. Bacon swore me to secrecy and I was freaking out because no one believed me about the body and I was just trying to figure out a way to prove that I saw what I saw and that it wasn't a hallucination."

"What did you see, Mistress Verity?"

"If I tell you, will you answer a question for me?"

"Tit for tat again, eh?"

"Uh, yeah. Can't we just call it an exchange of information? Or maybe quid pro quo?"

"Very well, but this time no leaving out the good stuff."

I have to stifle a shiver of revulsion upon hearing a dead body described as "the good stuff."

"And you go first," he says, "I want to hear about the body."

"Okay. There's not much to tell. She was lying on the floor in the passageway and it looked like someone had strangled her with one of King Henry's necklaces. I'm pretty sure it was Sarah Buckley, but since the body disappeared I have no proof and the police seem reluctant to take me seriously. Possibly because of the ketchup."

"Ketchup?"

"Never mind. So, yeah, that's it. She was in the passageway, she was definitely dead, and by the time King Henry showed up the body had disappeared."

"So you're the only one who saw her?"

"Yup. Okay, my turn," I say, and decide to go for broke. I look around the room. No one seems to be paying any attention to us, but there are enough people around that I feel comfortable asking Floyd what I'm about to ask him. "If you'd just killed Sarah in the secret passageway behind the alcove, where would you hide the body?"

I expect him to look shocked or something, but he just cocks his head to one side and taps a finger against his lips. "You ask such interesting questions, Mistress Verity. Let me see. How much time do I have?"

"Ten minutes tops. Probably more like six or seven. And I already know there are only two sets of stairs in the passageway, one leading down to the dungeon and one that leads up to Hank's private quarters."

"I see. Yes, upstairs or down. There's the cabinet..." His one beady eye suddenly lights up. "The priest hole, of course! But the King's bedchamber would be a risk. Too many chances for discovery. But the dungeon...there's the iron maiden, I suppose."

"The what?"

He smiles at me. It's a quick, triumphant grin and then just as suddenly it's replaced by a worried frown. "The priest hole or the iron maiden. But no one knows. Except..."

"Except what?"

"That's all I'm prepared to say, Sister Elizabeth. A secret is a very lucrative thing to have. Ask King Henry." He taps his nose and walks away.

Oh, sure. And I'm the crazy one.

"Your knight in shining armor, reporting for duty."

I look up to see Grayson in his billowy white shirt. He has got to stop looking like he just stepped off the cover of a romance novel. My heart can't take the exquisite torture. "What?" I say, forgetting whatever it was he just said.

"'I told you I would always come for you,'" he quotes, and I find myself desperately wishing we really were in a book and that this was a kissing scene. "Hey, are you okay? You look a little flustered."

Well, yeah. Stop being so heart-stoppingly dreamy. And stop making me wonder if you're saying these things because you love the same movie I do, or because you love *me*. "I'm fine. I was just thinking about something. What are you doing in here? Shouldn't you be galloping around on a horse or practicing left-handed sword fighting or whatever?"

"King Henry asked me to serve as your squire today. I'm supposed to escort you to the Oratory."

"He did?" I ask, feeling flustered. The plan was to ogle Grayson from *afar*, not up close and personal. Unrequited love is much easier to take from afar. "I thought you were training to be a knight?"

"His Majesty assures me this is a temporary assignment, just until he gets the Sarah Buckley Situation squared away."

"The Sarah Buckley Situation? Did he really call it that?"

"Yeah, he did. He called me into his study to ask

me if I thought you were nuts."

"Seriously? I thought he was on *my* side. Why is everyone so eager to assume I'm nuts? Just because I blurt out random bizarre statements and find dead bodies that disappear before anyone else sees them?"

"I think it was more that he wanted to make sure *I* was on your side. And when I assured him that you're mostly perfectly sane, he asked me if I'd keep an eye on you."

"So you're supposed to spy on me?" Something about this setup feels off.

"I'm not spying on you. I'd just like to make sure whoever killed Sarah doesn't come after you. Come on, Jules. I'm on your side."

"Fine. Let's go." I stand up.

He puts a hand on my arm, and the surge of warmth it sends through me conflicts with the icky feeling of having him assigned to be my spy. "Jules, I'll admit the psychic thing still kind of makes me nervous, but I really am on your side here. I want to help. Plus, I owe you one for accusing you of cheating on that math test. Let me help."

I look up at him, and my heart gives a funny little flutter. "The virgin hides the truth!" I yell in his face.

"You don't say?"

"I pretty much wish I hadn't."

*O*n the way to the Oratory, I fill Grayson in on the latest developments in the Sarah Buckley

Situation, including my interview with the police, Sarah's alleged larceny scheme, and my conversations with Jared and Floyd.

"Wow," Grayson says. "Sarah was stealing stuff?" He pauses at the Oratory door.

"Yeah, and the police think she had an accomplice. Hang on, let me check my schedule." I duck into the room and grab the sheet of paper on the wooden table. I have two private readings scheduled, both right before dinner. "I don't have anyone coming for a private reading for a while. Are you supposed to stand at the door or can you sit down and pretend to be a supplicant for the tourists?"

"My orders are to stand at the door and look deeply menacing to anyone who might wish you bodily harm."

"Gotcha."

"But I'm all ears if you want to talk."

My head and my heart are at war over the prospect of spending more time with Grayson, especially when it involves having to do my Maid of Kent act in front of him. I decide to focus on the Sarah Buckley Situation and ignore the Alone With a Hot Guy Situation.

"Okay, let me know if there's a group coming so I can hurry up and act pious." I move a chair closer to the door and grab the Maid of Kent's huge Bible. "From what the police said, it sounds like Sarah was probably working her way through Hank's collection of Tudor replicas. I wonder if she was on her way to replace the necklace when someone attacked her in the passageway? One of those sets of stairs leads to Hank's private quarters where he probably keeps the really expensive stuff. I bet that's how she got her hands on the replicas."

"You don't still think there's any chance Hank killed her, do you?"

"No. But we have to consider it as a possibility, right? It's his house, his employee, his jewelry."

"And if she was stealing his stuff that gives him a motive."

"Yeah. But if he killed Sarah, why would he call the police? The last thing he'd want is to have them sniffing around Tudor Times. And if he killed her because she was stealing his stuff, then he wouldn't need to call the police, because he would already know what she was up to, right?"

"Makes sense. So what are the police going to do?"

"Hank said he showed them the passageway and there was no evidence of foul play or anything. I guess they'll contact Sarah's friends and relatives and see if anyone's heard from her. Which, obviously they haven't since she's dead. What about Mike the Knight? You said they did Renaissance Faire stuff together. Is there any chance he could have been her accomplice?"

"It's possible. Listen to this, I asked him about Sarah when I saw him at the stables earlier today and he was really weird about it. He asked me why I thought he'd know what Sarah was up to and I said I thought they were friends, that they did the whole Ren Faire thing together, and he said, 'I don't keep tabs on Sarah. I have no idea what she's been up to.' He obviously didn't want to talk about her. And then I found out he took off right after we finished talking. He's gone. Didn't even bother to sign out."

"Weird. When I talked to him he asked me if Sarah had a weapon with her, specifically a jeweled dagger. Do you think the dagger was one of the replicas Sarah stole?"

"Could be. It definitely sounds suspicious."

"Right? Crap, I should have told the police about him."

"Okay, so King Henry is probably in the clear, but Mike is looking shady. What do you think about Floyd?"

"I don't know. He actually admitted to knowing about the secret passageway and purposely keeping secrets. And he told me where he'd hide the body, which he probably wouldn't do if he was the murderer, right? Which reminds me, do you have any idea what an iron maiden or a priest hole are?"

"You mean, besides the band?"

"The what?"

"Iron Maiden, eighties heavy metal band?"

"Yeah, I kind of doubt he was talking about a heavy metal band." I look sideways at Grayson. "Hank said we can't go in the passageway but he didn't say anything about the dungeon."

"I like the way you think, Buttercup." Grayson grins at me.

Happy sigh. Okay, refocus, Jules. "Except don't you think the police would have checked everywhere?

And I got the feeling Floyd was going to make a beeline for every possible place to stash a dead body as soon as we finished our conversation."

"Does that mean you don't want to look?"

"No, I do. I'm just guessing that if there was anything to be found Floyd will have already beaten us to it."

"Well, it can't hurt to check. As long as we stay out of Hank's private rooms. Which leaves the dungeon. Do you know how to get there without using the secret passageway?"

"Yeah, there's a staircase in the southeast corner of the castle."

"You're finished after you do your dinner performance, right? I say we do a little dungeon recon, what do you say?"

Chapter Twenty-Three

Away Inctersphay Ayssay Atwhay?

The day is going fairly well; no one has attempted to kill me and I've managed to make some decent premonitions and a few nonsensical butterfly blurts for the castle guests, and I've almost gotten over feeling like a total habit-wearing-spontaneous-blurter dork in front of Grayson, when I hear a voice in the hallway that makes me want to jump out of one of the Oratory's stained glass windows.

"Grayson, is that you? Oh. My. God. You look so hot! Doesn't he look hot, Whitney?"

"Totally droolsome. Bree is *so* lucky."

"Right? Is this where we go for our psychic reading? I know what I want in my future. Am I right, Whit?"

"Go right in, fair maidens. Sister Elizabeth awaits," Grayson says, and in walk Sidney Barlow and her bestie, Whitney Petty.

"Jules?" Sidney squeals. "Oh my God! You're a nun! That is so tragic. Whitney, look at her!"

Whitney gives a shiver of horror. "That's so totally gruesome."

"Hello, fair maidens," I say in my quiet, unperturbed Maid of Kent voice. "Are you here for a reading?" What I really want to say is, *Are you serious? Is this some kind of punishment from God for complaining about having to wear a nun outfit?* Because I can't think of two people I'd less like to see while playing the Maid of Kent. Sidney Barlow has had it out for me ever since the crimson wave incident, and it certainly doesn't help that my best friend is her drama club nemesis. Whitney Petty is just, well, petty.

"Bree said we had to come see you because you're like totally amazeballs or something," Sidney says.

"Yeah, like totally awesomesauce," Whitney adds.

"I see."

"So, what do you do, like read my palm or something?" Sidney asks.

"Have a seat, fair maidens, and I will see what the spirits have to say."

Sidney and Whitney sit down, and I close my eyes and try to decide how much I'm going to mess with them.

I open my eyes. "Which one of you is Sidney?" I ask.

"Duh, Jules. You know *I* am," Sidney says.

"Who is this 'Jules' you speak of? I am the Maid of Kent. You may call me Sister Elizabeth, if you wish. The spirits have a message for Sidney, would you like to hear it?"

"Well, yeah."

I give her a stern nunly look, and she shifts uncomfortably in her chair, then looks at Whitney, who shrugs.

"Yes, please, Sister Elizabeth."

"The rain in Spain stays mainly in the plain."

"It does? Oh my God! Does that mean I'm going to play Eliza Doolittle?"

"Do a little or do a lot, it will come to naught."

"What? What's that supposed to mean?"

"My task is to pass on the messages from the spirits. It is up to you to decipher what they mean to you."

"Fine. What other visions do you have for me then?"

"The spirits are finding it difficult to come through today." I put my fingers to my veil. "Oh, wait. They have another message: you seek to be a lady fair, but Camille will be the fairest of them all."

"Camille? You mean Cami?"

"Perhaps. Does this mean something to you?"

"It should mean something to *you*, she's *your* best friend."

"I have no friends. I am but a poor nun who has been blessed with the gift of visions."

"Fine. In your *vision* am I going to get the lead

in *My Fair Lady* or what? And what about senior prom? I'm going to be queen, right?"

I roll my eyes back in my head and mumble, "A sphincter says what?" in Pig Latin.

"What? What did you say?" Sidney demands.

"I told you she was a total freak," Whitney whispers.

"Hold on. I'm getting another vision." I squeeze my eyes shut and press my fingers to my temples. "You are dressed in a silken gown that glows like firelight. And there is something on your head. Something shiny and round. A crown? No, it's on your nose. It's...it's...it looks like...a giant pus-filled, plague-spreading bubo!" I open my eyes and smile serenely at Sidney.

"What the hell is a bubo?" she asks.

"I hope it's not like mono," Whitney says. "You'd think something called the kissing disease would be awesome but it's so not."

"You've never heard of the bubonic plague?" I ask, then add, "Don't worry, it's probably just a giant zit. I'm sure they can Photoshop it out of your prom pictures."

"You know what?" Sidney says, standing up. "I think you're full of crap, Jules Verity. I don't know why Bree likes you so much. You've always been a freak, and you always will be. Come on, Whit. We're out of here."

Sidney and Whitney storm out of the room, and I sit there trying not to giggle.

Grayson pokes his head in and gives me a funny

look. Then he starts laughing.

"I probably shouldn't have done that," I say.

"Are you kidding? That was 'totally amazeballs.'"

"I thought you were friends with Sidney."

"I tolerate her for Bree's sake. But just because Bree's capable of being friends with everyone she meets doesn't mean I want to be. I don't have her gift for seeing the good in everyone. And I definitely can't see what she sees in Sidney Barlow."

"Oh, come on. Sidney's totally up on the latest fashion trends, has perfectly manicured fingernails, and not a split end in sight. What more could you want?"

"A lot. How about someone who's unrelentingly honest, appealingly quirky, and a fan of the best movie ever?" Grayson takes a step toward me.

"Those sound good," I say, and my breath catches in my throat as he steps even closer.

"Or how about someone who's totally unaware of her own beauty?" Grayson says and his eyes drift to my lips. "Someone who likes to wear cherry-red lip gloss?"

I reach a hand up to touch my lips. If I didn't know that Grayson already had the most perfect girlfriend ever... But no. There's no way Grayson could ever want *me*. Could he? He takes another step closer and we're inches apart and I'm having very un-nunly thoughts when a tour group appears in the doorway behind Grayson. "Greetings lords and ladies!" I exclaim, sounding like an overzealous salesclerk.

Grayson stiffens, then turns without a word to take up his post at the door.

Chapter Twenty-Four

A Little Dungeon Recon

I'm not sure if I'm relieved or disappointed that there are no more moments alone with Grayson. My next private reading is pretty anticlimactic after the drama with Sidney. I talk to an elderly woman wearing a T-shirt that reads "Keep Calm and Weed On" about her garden for twenty minutes, and then it's time to go to the minstrel gallery to prepare for my dinner performance.

I spot a family wearing matching Disneyland shirts and decide to make some kind of premonition involving princesses and mice in red shorts, but when I enter the Great Hall and King Henry asks me if I have a message for someone present I blurt out, "Mermaids blush when clothes unmake the man!"

"Blushing mermaids, how delightful," King

Henry responds, but he looks a little nervous. "And who, may I ask, is this message for?"

"Um," I look desperately around the Hall, "the spirits are very mysterious tonight. The message will be received by the one it is meant for." I can already feel another blurt building.

King Henry seems to sense my unease. "Thank you, Sister Elizabeth. Perhaps the spirits will be more—"

"No amount of bathing will ever make him clean!" I shout, and then make for the back doors feeling like I've just let loose the equivalent of a psychic fart. I'm anxious to avoid letting another one escape, lest I say something else about naked men. Or unmade men, or whatever the hell I said.

Grayson is waiting outside the doors to the Great Hall.

"Blushing mermaids, eh? You know you're going to get the 'this is a family establishment' lecture for the naked guy comment, right?"

"I didn't say anyone was naked! And don't you think it's a bit hypocritical for a guy portraying a king who goes around beheading everyone to be concerned about offending people?"

"Hey, I'm on your side, remember?"

"Do you have any idea how horrible it is to yell things out without having the slightest idea what you're going to say?"

"Nope. But I can think of something that might be equally horrible."

"What?"

"Searching a dungeon for a dead body?"

"Fine. Let's just get it over with."

I lead the way to the staircase that descends to the dungeon.

"You sure you still want to do this?" Grayson asks, putting a hand on my arm.

"No, but at least I know you're not going to go into labor like Angelique." I hand him the LED candle I borrowed from the Oratory. "After you."

"Just promise me Count Rugen isn't down there waiting to hook me up to the Machine, okay?" Grayson says, and laughs nervously.

"No Count Rugen, I promise. But I can't say the same about torture devices."

"Or dead bodies?"

"Or dead bodies."

Grayson gives my arm a squeeze, then flicks on the candle and starts down the stairs.

I pull out my flashlight/stun gun and loop the cord around my wrist, then hit the flashlight button. We're halfway down the steep winding staircase when it starts to sink in that I'm on a covert mission with Grayson Chandler to a dungeon in a castle where someone was probably strangled to death.

This is so not how I thought I was going to be spending my summer.

"You ready?" Grayson asks when we get to the bottom of the stairs.

"I guess so."

"Okay, then. Let's go find an iron maiden."

Grayson pulls up the heavy wooden bar and

opens the door. "Is there a light switch in here, do you think?" he asks as we enter the dimly lit dungeon.

We search the wall next to the door and I find a metal wall sconce like the one in the secret passageway. I twist the button and the room goes from dim to slightly less dim.

"There's another one over here," Grayson says and turns on a second wall sconce.

I click off my flashlight but keep my finger over the stun gun button just in case. I point to the large wooden cabinet on the far wall. "Inside the cabinet is the hidden entrance to the passageway. There's a set of stairs that lead to the ground floor and the passageway behind the alcove in the main hallway." We look around the room for obvious hiding places.

"What's that?" Grayson asks, pointing to the wood and iron statue in the corner.

"That's the Virgin of Nuremberg," I say. "Angelique says it's—"

"Wait, did you say 'virgin'?" Grayson asks.

I nod.

"As in, 'the virgin hides the truth'?" He walks over to the statue.

"You're putting way too much faith in my blurts."

"There's a plaque here that says it's the Iron Maiden of Nuremberg."

"But no mention of virgins?"

"Nope."

We both stare at the iron maiden.

"It's certainly big enough to hide a body," I offer.

"True. Okay. So. We should probably open it,

right?"

"Yeah. But only if we want to see what's inside."

Grayson reaches out and grabs the iron handle next to the studded strip of iron that looks almost like a row of buttons running down the center of the maiden's dress.

"Here goes nothing," he says.

"I'm sure the police have already looked in here," I say.

He pulls the handle, and the right half of the maiden's dress swings open with an ominous creaking noise. And Floyd Bean lurches out at me.

In a panic I bring my stun gun up and hit the juice. Floyd's body jerks violently as we both fall to the ground. He lands on top of me, pinning my stun gun arm between us. I scream and push at him with my free hand but he's like a dead weight on top of me. And then Grayson grabs him and I kick at Floyd with all my might as Grayson rolls him off of me.

"Jules, stop. He's dead."

I freeze and look up at Grayson. "What?"

"I'm pretty sure he's dead. Look at him."

I sit up and look at Floyd. And see the jeweled dagger sticking out of his chest.

"Oh my God. Oh my God, Grayson. He's been stabbed."

Grayson kneels down and puts his fingers on Floyd's throat where his pulse should be.

"Yeah, he's dead. We need to call the police."

"I'm not leaving him," I say.

"What?"

"I'm not leaving him. I'm not taking a chance on him disappearing like Sarah did."

"Jules, we have to go get help. And there's no way I'm leaving you down here by yourself. He's not going to disappear. And even if he did, I can vouch for the fact that he was here."

I look back at Floyd. There are drops of red spilling from the front of his uniform, and at first I think I'm looking at blood. I scooch closer for a better look. "Grayson, look." I point to what I now realize are jewels spilling out of his pocket. I reach into the pocket and pull out a handful of rubies and pearls.

"What the hell?" Grayson says. "Are those real?"

"I don't know. If they are, they could be the jewels Sarah stole."

"Yeah, but what does that mean? Floyd killed her for the jewels?"

"Or maybe he was her accomplice?"

"My money was on Mike the Knight, but what's Floyd doing with all those jewels? And if he's her accomplice, who killed *him*?"

"Whoever killed him used a jeweled dagger," I point out. "It can't possibly be a coincidence that Mike asked me if Sarah had a jeweled dagger, can it? But if Sarah had the dagger... I have no idea what that means."

We both stare at Floyd. His face looks worn, his cheeks sunken and creased with age. It's hard to picture him as a murderer. Creepy? Yes. But murderer? Not so much.

"Are you sure Sarah was dead?" Grayson asks,

and I feel a shiver run through me.

"You think she killed him?"

"I don't know. This is all way out of my league."

"She was dead, Grayson. I'm sure of it."

"We need to call the police," Grayson says again. He holds out a hand to help me up, and then we both stand there looking down at Floyd. "You know what's weird? I could swear I saw him move. It was like he jumped on top of you. There's no way he was still alive, is there?"

I hold up my lipstick stun gun. "I zapped him."

"You what? I thought that was a flashlight."

"It is." I push the flashlight button and then the button for the stun gun. A blue spark crackles between the two points on the tip of the faux lipstick canister. "It's also a stun gun. Gran made me promise to carry it at all times. And I thought Floyd was attacking me," I explain, "so I zapped him."

"Understandable. Remind me never to mess with you, okay?"

*A*n hour later the police are processing the crime scene and I'm sitting in Hank's study waiting to be "debriefed." Grayson has been taken to an adjoining room and, I assume, awaits a similar fate.

There's a brief knock at the door and Officer Kilbride strolls in. "Miss Verity, we meet again," he says and sits down next to me on the couch. He puts a hand on my shoulder. "How are you holding up?"

"The body's still there, right? You saw it?"

"The body is still there. The coroner is getting ready to take it away, but if the body somehow manages to disappear en route we have photographic proof that it existed and that Mr. Bean was, indeed, dead."

I can't help it, I let loose a sigh of relief.

Officer Kilbride takes out his notebook. "Why don't you tell me what happened this time?"

"Sure. We were looking for Sarah's body in the dungeon and we found Floyd instead."

"I see. And how did you know where to look?"

"I didn't. It was a guess. I was trying to figure out what happened to Sarah after I found her and she disappeared. Where someone could have taken her body. It just didn't make sense. And it didn't seem like you guys were looking all that hard for her. Floyd knew the castle better than anyone so I asked him where *he* would have hidden Sarah."

"And what did he tell you, Miss Verity? Did he give you a location where he thought the body might be?"

"Yes. Two, actually. One was upstairs in Mr. Bacon's private rooms, so I obviously couldn't go there."

"And the other?"

"Was the iron maiden. I had no idea what he was talking about but I knew whatever it was was in the dungeon, and I'd promised not to go in the secret passageway but as far as I knew the dungeon wasn't off-limits, so Grayson and I decided to see if we could find the iron maiden."

"Grayson Chandler? Your high school classmate?"

"Yes. Hank temporarily appointed him as my personal squire-slash-bodyguard."

"I see. So, Floyd told you the iron maiden would be a good place to hide a body and hours later he turns up, dead, inside it?"

"Yeah, pretty much. Grayson pulled open her dress and Floyd came tumbling out."

"I see. That must have been quite a surprise."

"Yeah. It was. I should probably mention that I zapped him."

"You what?"

I pull my lipstick stun gun out of my pocket and offer it to Officer Kilbride. "It's a stun gun. Gran made me promise to carry it with me at all times. I have a note from her saying I have permission. It's in my cubby if you want to see it."

Officer Kilbride flips the cap off and examines the stun gun. "Our ME might need to take a look at this, but for now I suggest you follow your Gran's advice. You seem to have a habit of stumbling over dead bodies, Miss Verity."

"It's really not my favorite thing. But at least Floyd's didn't disappear."

"That brings up an interesting point, Miss Verity. You're the only one who's seen Sarah Buckley dead."

"Uh, no. I'm pretty sure whoever killed her and moved her body saw her, too."

"What I'm saying, Miss Verity, is that we only have your assumption that Sarah Buckley is dead. And now we have the body of someone who, based on the preliminary evidence found on his person, would appear to have been involved in Miss Buckley's larceny scheme, but still no Miss Buckley. Has it occurred to you that Sarah Buckley might be the person responsible for Floyd's death?"

"Yeah, except for the fact that that's impossible. Because she's dead."

"Shall we discuss Officer Lasky's theory then? If Sarah Buckley isn't the killer, guess who the second most likely suspect is? Someone who knows about the secret passageways and the best places to hide a body." He raises an eyebrow at me.

"Mike the Knight?" I say, hopefully.

"Who's Mike the Knight?"

"I forgot to tell you about him. He's a friend of Sarah's. They're in the same Renaissance guild. Anyway, he heard me asking about Sarah and wanted to know if I'd seen her and if she'd been carrying any weapons, specifically a jeweled dagger."

"I see. And why didn't you mention this before?"

"I told you, I forgot. I was kind of flustered, what with the whole murder and interrogation thing. Not to mention Officer Lasky's 'theory.' I mean, seriously? Why would I tell everyone I found a body and then hide it?"

"I don't believe you did."

"Okay, I'm confused."

"Officer Lasky thinks perhaps Miss Buckley needed to disappear, and you helped her do that."

"And then I killed Floyd and conveniently 'found' him, too, so I could call the police and you could make up another ridiculous scenario? So, according to Officer Lasky, I'm not only guilty of larceny and murder, I'm also moronically stupid. Is that correct?"

"Miss Verity, I'm not accusing you of anything. But the facts don't add up."

"The facts seem pretty clear to me. Sarah Buckley is dead and so is Floyd Bean, and I didn't kill either of them. You should probably start trying to figure out who did before they kill someone else and stick them in the priest hole, whatever that is."

"The priest hole?"

"That's the other hiding place Floyd told me about. It's somewhere in Mr. Bacon's private rooms."

"Interesting. Why don't we get Mr. Bacon in here and ask him about it?" Officer Kilbride goes to the door and tells the officer stationed there to ask Mr. Bacon to join us.

We sit in silence, Officer Kilbride flipping through his notes, as we wait for Hank.

When he comes in a few minutes later he stands by the door as if reluctant to be a part of the proceedings.

"Yes, Officer Kilbride? I understand you require my presence?"

"Yes, have a seat please, Mr. Bacon."

Hank sits down in one of the chairs across from the couch.

"Miss Verity has been telling me some information she learned from Floyd Bean before his untimely demise. He claimed there was a 'priest hole' somewhere in your personal quarters. Are you aware of such a thing?"

"A priest hole? Truly? It wouldn't surprise me. As I continue to learn, old Mr. Lune was very much a man who liked secrets, and a priest hole would be a very appropriate addition to a Tudor castle if there wasn't one built into it already."

"I'm not familiar with the term. Would you mind enlightening us as to what it refers to?"

"Certainly. A priest hole is the name given to a secret room or hiding place that was meant to allow a Catholic priest who was fleeing persecution during Elizabeth I's reign to evade capture. Many castles and country homes in England already had secret passageways that would allow them to escape at a moment's notice. These were very uncertain times, you see. But after Elizabeth I became queen, many Catholic households created secret rooms intended to hide practicing priests, hence the name 'priest hole' came about."

"I see, and is it possible there is one of these priest holes somewhere in your personal quarters?"

"Why don't we go find out?" Hank says and launches himself out of his chair before Officer Kilbride can respond. He holds out a hand to me. "Mistress Verity? Would you care to accompany us?"

"I don't think—" Officer Kilbride begins to protest, but Hank cuts him off.

"Unless I am mistaken, my personal quarters are not part of your crime scene, Officer Kilbride. And if you would like to investigate them without a search warrant, I suggest you indulge me."

Chapter Twenty-Five
The Priest Hole

We all troop up the stairs to Hank's private rooms, pulling aside a velvet rope with a small hand-lettered sign that says No Entry. Hank uses a large metal key to unlock the huge wooden doors leading to his bedroom. The room looks the way I imagine it would have in the sixteenth century, with no sign of modern amenities despite the fact that it's off-limits to everyone but Hank. On the far wall is an enormous intricately carved oak bed hung with velvet curtains; the walls are covered in beautiful golden tapestries and the floor with colorful woven rugs. The ceiling is magnificent, painted blue and gold and adorned with golden cherubs who gaze down on us with blissful expressions.

"Okay, if you were a priest hole, where would you

be?" I ask Hank.

"It could be a man-sized space under the floor somewhere, or an actual room hidden behind paneling, a piece of furniture, or possibly a fireplace."

We all look around the room, which is fairly sparsely furnished. Apart from the bed there are a few velvet-padded chairs, a heavily carved table, a huge buffet, and a painted wood cabinet. Hank walks over to a large painting hanging on one of the walls, Officer Kilbride starts tapping on the wall paneling, and I walk over to the enormous fireplace, which features an inner carved stone section surrounded by a beautiful carved wood overmantel that reaches all the way to the ceiling. The inside of the fireplace is gray stone and I bend down to get a closer look. It doesn't look as though anyone has lit a fire inside it in a long time. I step back and look at the wooden overmantel. In the center is a crest surmounted by cherubs, with columns on either side. I run my fingers over the intricate carving, not sure what I'm looking for. Another secret mechanism?

Unlike seemingly everyone else, I don't have the slightest doubt about whether or not Sarah is dead. But after finding Floyd, I'm no longer sure I *want* to find Sarah's body. At least not personally. I've had more than my share of contact with dead people over the last couple of days, and the last thing I want is to find myself writhing around on the ground underneath another corpse.

Staring at the cherubs brings back a wisp of memory. Something I blurted recently but immediately tried to forget because it was no doubt embarrassing, ill-timed, or just plain bizarre. At the top of the wooden crest, flanked by the cherubs, sits a crown. At the apex of the crown, the wood is carved to resemble a faceted jewel, and I spot what looks like a crack along the edge, so I pull a velvet chair over to get a closer look. The crack appears deliberate as it goes all the way around the base of the decoration. I take a deep breath and push on the jewel. I swear it depresses slightly, but nothing else happens.

"Well done, Mistress Verity!" Hank booms, and I look around in confusion. He points at the inside of the fireplace.

I hop off my chair and take a look. The back wall of the fireplace has slid to the side, revealing a small room beyond. "Holy crap!"

"An appropriate sentiment for a priest hole, one might say," Hank says, striding toward the opening.

"Hold on, Mr. Bacon," Officer Kilbride says. "There may be important evidence in there."

"Evidence of what? If there was a body in there we would have smelled it by now, Officer Kilbride."

I realize he's right, and I feel both relieved and disappointed. I want the mystery of Sarah's disappearance to be solved, but I could do without the decomposing corpse part.

Hank ducks to enter the space behind the fireplace and gives a low whistle. "Well, Miss Buckley may not be here now but she certainly has been before."

I scramble through the opening to take a peek

before Officer Kilbride can stop me. The room is small, about five feet square. Against one wall is a narrow wooden table cluttered with photographs of jewelry pieces, small jars of gemstones and pearls, various tools and jewelry-making supplies, a flashlight, a disposable coffee cup, and a copy of Philippa Gregory's *The Queen's Fool* lying splayed open.

"All right, both of you, out of there," Officer Kilbride says, and I step back through the opening. Hank follows behind me and Officer Kilbride takes his place inside the little room. He looks around for a moment or two before unclipping his police radio. "Hey, Joe. I'm going to need an evidence team up on the second floor," he says and describes our location. He steps out of the priest hole and gives me a hard look. "So, you had no idea this place was here, huh?"

"I've never been in this room before."

"My private quarters are off-limits to the staff," Hank says. "I have the only key, which I thought, until recently, meant I was the only one with access." He walks over to the heavy wooden wardrobe. "I've since discovered there is an entrance to one of the secret passageways inside this wardrobe. Which must be how Miss Buckley gained access to my collection of Tudor artifacts and reproductions. I assume, based on what we've just seen, that she used the priest hole as her workspace. I am rarely up here during the day, so it wouldn't be difficult for her to avoid detection."

"And you've since moved your collections to a more secure location, correct?"

"Correct. Everything of value has been removed until I can have a vault installed in the room next door."

"Thank you, Mr. Bacon. I'm afraid we're going to be here a while longer. If you'd like to make yourself comfortable someplace else I'll supervise things up here."

"Am I free to go?" I ask.

"Yes, Miss Verity. But I'll be in touch."

While Officer Kilbride and his team get ready to do their *CSI* thing, Hank and I head back downstairs. Grayson is waiting outside Hank's study.

"There you are," he says when he sees me. "Are we allowed to go now?" he asks Hank.

"I'd like a word first," Hank says and leads us into his study. Grayson and I sit on opposite sides of the room while Hank takes a seat behind his desk. "I don't know what's going on in this castle, but obviously I am deeply disturbed by the death of Floyd and the disappearance and possible death of Sarah Buckley. I do not want any more lives lost under my watch. Mistress Verity, I know we may disagree on this, but I trust Officer Kilbride to do his job. Which means I don't want you doing it. No more lurking around the castle looking for clues or secret passageways, or places to stash dead bodies, understood?"

I nod.

"You, too, Mr. Chandler. I am disappointed in you. Your job was to keep Mistress Verity safe, not lead her into the bowels of the castle looking for murder victims. If I catch either of you doing anything other than the jobs I've hired you to do, you will be terminated."

I wince at his choice of words.

"Fired. You will be fired on the spot. Understood?"

"Understood," Grayson and I chorus.

"Fine. Assuming the police are able to wrap up their investigation by opening time, I will see you tomorrow," Hank says. "Mistress Verity, I called your grandmother and assured her you are still in one piece. Do not make a liar out of me."

"I won't. Thank you, sir."

Chapter Twenty-Six

Everything Is Going to Be Peachy Keen

As we head for the staff parking lot, I can't help wondering what it's like for Hank after we all go home and he's alone in the castle. And tonight he'll be truly alone. With Floyd dead, the gatehouse, Floyd's caretaker home, will be empty.

"Do you think he'll be okay?" I ask Grayson as I slide into the passenger seat of his SUV.

"Who? Hank?"

"Yeah. It's got to be creepy being here all alone at night. Especially knowing there's more than likely a dead body somewhere on the premises."

"He's not alone. The police will probably be here for hours."

"Yeah, I guess you're right. But Officer Kilbride

isn't exactly good company. Or maybe it's just that he doesn't like me."

"Why wouldn't he like you?"

"He has an aversion to psychic nuns?" I suggest, and then shrug. "I have no idea." But really I know why. Officer Kilbride knows I'm hiding something. Something that makes me feel ridiculously guilty. I'm guessing he thinks it's something more sinister than being in love with someone else's boyfriend. "Where's Bree?" I say, following up on that train of thought.

"She got a ride home with Kaitlyn again. I told her I'd call her as soon as the police let us go. She was pretty freaked."

"Yeah, I imagine everyone's going to be freaked when they hear. We found the priest hole, by the way."

"You did? Where was it? *What* was it? I assume there was no body inside?"

I fill him in on Sarah's hidden lair.

"Jeez, this place is full of secrets."

"I know," I say. Just like me. I look over at Grayson. He's focused on the road ahead, and I take advantage of the opportunity to ogle him up close. The way his hair curls around his ears, the slight dimple in his chin, how his bottom lip looks so incredibly kissable...

"What?" Grayson says, looking over at me.

"I'm sorry," I say, blushing deeply.

"What? Why?"

"I'm sorry I got you involved in all this," I say,

even though I'm not. I mean, of course I'm horribly sorry two people are dead, but I'm not sorry for this time I've had with Grayson. For the realization that he no longer seems to think I'm a weirdo to be avoided at all costs. I *am* sorry he has a girlfriend and that she's someone so perfect I can't even begrudge her her phenomenal luck at being the girlfriend of the most perfect boy I've ever met.

"It's not your fault, Jules."

Yes, it is, I want to say, but don't. If he hadn't been working at Tudor Times I would have never taken the job as the Maid of Kent. And I would have never involved him in this mess.

We're both quiet for the rest of the drive to my house.

"Thanks for the ride," I say as we pull to a stop.

"Jules, are you okay? I mean, of course you're not, you got tackled by a dead guy, but...you're going to be okay, right?"

"Eventually," I say. But I'm not thinking about Floyd or Sarah or any of the rest of the Tudor Times mess. That stuff is all horrifically awful, but it feels survivable. I'm thinking about my heart and how I'm never going to get it back from Grayson Chandler no matter how hard I try. I reach for the door handle.

"Don't go, Jules," he says and puts a hand on my arm.

I look down at his hand, confused.

"I...I want to..." He can't seem to get the words out, and when I look at his face his expression lets loose a kaleidoscope of butterflies in my chest. "Jules," he says urgently as he leans toward me and I swear he's going to kiss me and I start to lean in and then...

I pull away. "You'd better go call Bree. She'll be worried."

He straightens up and puts both hands on the steering wheel. "Yeah, I will. Pick you up at twelve thirty tomorrow?"

I'm so confused. But I know I should tell him no. That I'll borrow my mom's van or drive Rosie. Instead I open my mouth to say, *Thanks, Grayson. I'd love a ride,* but then he gives me a sad smile and says, "I'm sorry, Jules. This is all such a mess."

My heart does that weird fluttering thing again and I say, "I don't need a ride. My mom says I can use her van until I get my bike fixed. Go call Bree." And I jump out of the car and run up the driveway before I can change my mind.

"There you are!" Cami pounces on me when I reach the porch. "Where've you been? What's going on at Tudor Times? I heard there were police cars there. Did they find the body?"

I hold up my hand. "Cami, please stop. I just can't right now."

Miraculously, she shuts up.

"Well, you've had a day," Gran says when I walk through the door. She looks from me to Cami. "Miss Cami, why don't you make us all some hot chocolate?"

"Sure," Cami says and gives my arm a squeeze before heading for the kitchen.

"Hank said he called you?"

"Yes. He called to let me know you were okay and

that you'd be home a bit late. Then that old biddy Esther Davis called to see if I had the inside scoop on the latest gossip, what with you working at Tudor Times. And Shirley Ferndale called wanting to know if it's true you can talk to the dead now and if so could you please find out where her Milton hid the savings bonds before he died? I swear the people in this town have no sense."

"If I could talk to the dead I wouldn't be in this mess."

"Isn't that the truth. Someone killed old Floyd Bean, eh? Stuck his nose where it didn't belong, I bet."

"Yeah. Or else he was Sarah Buckley's accomplice and she killed him. Or I'm her accomplice and I killed him for her. It's all starting to blend together."

"That's just silly. Sarah Buckley is dead."

"Well, duh. I've told the police that several times, but they seem to be having a hard time believing me without an actual body around. I only found Floyd because I was trying to prove Sarah was dead by finding *her* body for them."

"You found Floyd? Oh, honey. Your day was worse than I thought. Come here." She envelops me in a warm hug, and I breathe in the scent of her. She smells like Oil of Olay and violets and safety.

I don't mean to, but I start crying and pretty soon I'm out-and-out sobbing. "I'm...sorry. It's... not...I'm...just—"

"Don't try to talk, honey. Just let it all out."

Gran grabs me a box of Kleenex, and I cry

until I've used up half the box on the tears and snot streaming down my face.

"I'm not crying for Floyd," I finally say, between dwindling sobs.

"I know you're not."

"I don't know what to do. I didn't sign up to be the body finder. How can they not believe me that Sarah's dead? I know Officer Kilbride is suspicious of me because he knows I'm hiding something. But the thing I'm hiding has nothing to do with Sarah or Floyd or Tudor Times at all. And I can't really be a suspect in a double homicide, or a jewel forgery scam, or whatever the hell is going on, because that's ridiculous."

"I know, honey."

"I'm crying because I'm completely stressed out and I'm in love with Grayson. And I can't have him. And it's not *fair*."

"Life isn't fair, cupcake."

"Really? Is that what you tell your matchmaking clients?"

"Of course not, they actually listen to me."

"I listen to you."

"Well then, 'You have to accept whatever comes, and the only important thing is that you meet it with courage and with the best that you have to give.'"

"Really? You're going with an Eleanor Roosevelt quote? That's so not what I need to hear right now."

"I know. You want me to tell you that you and Grayson are a perfect match and that everything is going to be peachy keen."

"Well, yeah. That'd be nice."

"Love is hard work, kiddo. Even if you're lucky enough to find your soul mate."

"It's a lot harder when your soul mate already has a soul mate."

"I think you need to be patient, Juliet. Things have a way of working out."

"Yeah. Great. Whatever. I'll just forget Grayson and marry Prince Humperdinck."

"Who's Prince Humperdinck?"

I give an exasperated sigh. "Never mind. Let's go have some hot chocolate before Cami burns it again."

"You need to call your mother."

"You told her about Floyd?"

"No, but she's going to find out sooner or later. It would be better if she heard it from you."

"Gran, I just can't right now. She's going to freak out and— Can I please call her tomorrow? It's like five in the morning there, she won't be coherent anyway."

"Fine. But you need to call her first thing in the morning, hear me?"

"First thing," I promise.

I bring Cami and Gran up to date on all things Tudor Times, including Sidney and Whitney's visit to the Maid of Kent.

"You didn't!" Cami squeals when I tell her about the reading I gave Sidney.

"I did. And Grayson heard the whole thing."

"He did? What did he say?"

"Basically, that he can't stand Sidney either."

"Seriously? But she and Bree are total besties. Maybe he's preparing for their breakup."

"What breakup?"

"Grayson and Bree. When he finally realizes he hates her friends and secretly wants to be with you."

I grab her arm. "Cami, listen to me. You have to stop that."

"But Jules! It's so obvious that he—"

"Cami, I'm serious. I will never be Bree Blair, and I'm not going to be the kind of girl who goes after someone else's boyfriend, either. So stop. I don't want to talk about Grayson. Or your delusional conviction that he's in love with me. I can't be around him and have that in my head. It's too much for both my hormones and my heart."

"Fine. But you're every bit as awesome as Bree Blair. And someday, someone every bit as awesome as Grayson Chandler is going to see that."

"Thanks, Cami. And I love you, but you make the worst hot chocolate ever. So if you'll excuse me, I'm going to go to my room to play angsty music super loud."

"Fine. I'm going to go practice singing 'The Rain in Spain.'" Cami gives me a quick hug and takes off.

I pour my hot chocolate in the sink. "How do you even screw up hot chocolate?" I ask Gran.

"She has a gift. Please wear your headphones, dear. And remember, 'With the new day comes new strength and new thoughts.'"

"Yeah, and, 'Never go in against a Sicilian when death is on the line.'"

Chapter Twenty-Seven
He's My Buddy

When I tell my mom about Floyd the next morning she, predictably, freaks out.

"I'm calling Hank again," she says.

"I'm fairly certain that if he could prevent anyone else from getting killed, just to avoid another phone call from you, he would. Besides, the murderer doesn't need to kill me. I'm pretty sure the police think I'm a suspect."

"*What?*"

Oops. "Did I not mention that part? They think Sarah, the dead girl, had an accomplice, and who better than the daughter of an antique shop owner who could use her connections to sell stolen jewels for her daughter."

"My connections? What connections?"

"Right? And why would you tell Hank his necklace was fake if you were in on it? I mean, unless I hadn't told you about my jewel replacement scheme yet."

"Does anyone else know about this?"

"What? That I might be a murderer and a thief?"

"Juliet Hope Verity, this is not funny. My business is very important to me and I can't have—"

"Your *business*? Are you serious? I'm having nightmares about dead people and you're worried about your business?"

"That is not what I said."

"Well, clearly you and Dad care way more about gallivanting off to foreign lands and going through other people's stuff than you do about me."

"Don't you dare lump me in with your father. This is the first time I've been out of the country for work since we moved to Lunevale. And do you know one of the reasons I took this job, Juliet?"

"No. Why?" I ask, even though several answers come to mind: Europe has way better old stuff than America, spending the summer in France is clearly superior to spending it in Lunevale, etcetera.

"I took this job so we could use the extra money to buy you a car."

"Oh." Holy Guilt Trip on a Stick.

"So don't you dare imply that my work is more important to me than my family. If my business is going to be implicated in some kind of jewelry theft, of course I'm concerned. That business is the primary means of financial support for our family."

"You're right. I'm sorry." I should know better

than to underestimate my mom.

She lets out a gusty sigh. "But there won't be much of our family left if you get yourself killed and I go to jail for killing both Gran and Hank Bacon for not keeping you safe."

"Oh, come on. I've got a stun gun and a knight in shining armor to protect me. What could go wrong?" I say in an attempt to lighten things up.

"Who's this knight in shining armor?"

"Well, technically he's a squight, but only because he isn't eighteen yet. Don't worry, I'm sure he's a badass with a sword. Both right- and left-handed."

"Juliet, what are you talking about?"

"Hank assigned me a bodyguard." I don't tell her that I'm hoping to get him unassigned as soon as I get to work. My goal is to stay as far away from Grayson as possible until my brain finally convinces my heart that he's truly off-limits.

"Oh. Good. I'm going to call Hank and remind him that I will eviscerate him if anything happens to you."

"Okay, good luck with that. Tell him I can't wait until he's my new stepdaddy."

"Wait, what? What did you just say?"

"Auras never lie! I would totally throw down an Eleanor Roosevelt quote right now but I've purged them all from my brain."

"You know what? I don't even want to know."

"Good choice."

"Be careful, Jules. And call me if you need me. I can be on the next plane home."

"I'm fine, Mom."

"Good, because if you get yourself killed I'm going to eviscerate you, too."

"That doesn't really make sense, Mom."

"Good-bye, Jules. I love you very much."

"Love you, too."

When I arrive at Tudor Times, I'm told that Hank wants to talk to everyone before we begin our shifts. I get changed into my Maid of Kent costume and report to the Great Hall. I find an empty seat at one of the long tables and listen to the whispering going on around me.

"Someone killed Floyd?"

"Yeah, they found him in the dungeon."

"I heard they found another dead body in a secret passageway."

"No way! There are secret passageways? That's awesome!"

"I heard the new nun found the body."

"Good people, may I have your attention, please?" Hank booms. "I am afraid I have some rather shocking news." He waits until everyone settles down and gives him their full attention. "I am deeply saddened to tell you that Floyd Bean, or as he liked to call himself, the Keeper, is no longer with us. His body was discovered yesterday evening in the basement of the castle." He pauses and looks at us all and I see the deep sadness in his eyes. "He appears to have been the victim of foul play."

This announcement is followed by gasps and murmurs of alarm.

"We are also concerned about the whereabouts of Sarah Buckley, our Wardrobe Mistress. She has not been seen since late Friday. The police have set up an interview room in the Buttery, and they will be calling each of you in over the course of the day. Please give them your full cooperation so that we may resolve this terrible situation and achieve a measure of justice for the Keeper."

People are starting to look around at one another as if assessing who might be responsible for Sarah's disappearance and Floyd's death.

"In the meantime, I am instituting a new security policy. No one, at any time, is to be allowed anywhere in the castle alone. If you have a position that requires you to complete a task you have previously done alone, you have been assigned a buddy. The list of buddies has been posted in the staff dining room. Until we get to the bottom of this tragedy, you will make sure your buddy is never alone. Understood?"

There are murmurs of assent, although not everyone looks happy about this turn of events. Which is not all that surprising, given that it involves a fellow employee being stabbed to death.

"Dude. How do we know our buddy isn't the person who killed the Keeper?" someone behind me whispers.

"All right, everyone," Hank tells us. "You may return to work. Check the buddy list and if you have

any questions or concerns, be sure to voice them to
the police during your individual interview."

The room is buzzing with excitement and
speculation. I wonder if anyone will quit for fear of
being the next victim. I look around the room and am
surprised to see Angelique sitting at one of the other
tables. She gives me a wave and makes her way over
to me.

"What are you doing here?" I ask. "Are you
coming back to work already?"

She laughs and pats the tiny bundle nestled on
her chest. "Nope. I came to pick up my last paycheck.
I'm taking this little guy to San Francisco."

"You are? Oh my gosh, can I steal a peek at him?"

"Augustus Theodore, meet Jules Verity," she
says, pulling aside a bit of fabric so I can see the tiny
baby face inside.

"He's beautiful."

"I know." She grins, then her expression grows
serious. "Damn. Things have gotten crazy around
here, huh?"

"Yeah, they have."

She must see something in my face, because she
says, "Let's walk. I never got the chance to say good-
bye to the Oratory. And I have a confession to make."

We head out of the Great Hall and down the
hallway to the stairs. I avoid looking at the alcove
with the suit of armor as we pass by.

Angelique waves and smiles and calls greetings
to people on our way down the hall, but as soon as
we're in the Oratory she shuts the door and leads me

to a chair. "Sit. Tell me what's going on with you."

"Oh, you know. Just doing the nun thing."

"Don't bullshit me, Jules. Sarah's obviously the girl you saw in the passageway."

"Yup. Except I'm the only one who seems to think she's dead."

"Yeah, I heard about her stealing Hank's jewels and replacing them with fakes. Not a bad scam."

"Seriously? That's your take on it?"

"Well, killing people is going too far. Obviously."

"The police think she had an accomplice. It looks like it might have been Floyd, but if Sarah's dead, then who killed him?"

"Good question."

"Also, the police think I'm hiding something and that I'm somehow involved in Sarah's scheme."

"Are you?"

"I'm so not. I'd never even met Sarah before I found her in the passageway. But they're not taking me seriously because of the whole blurting thing."

"Not cool."

"Yeah, it really sucks."

There's a knock at the door and it starts to open before Angelique or I have a chance to get up.

"There you are, buddy," Grayson says, smiling at me. He's wearing his flowy white shirt and tights and I'm pretty sure a small sigh escapes me. "You're not supposed to go anywhere without me."

"What?" I say, wondering if I'm daydreaming. I look over at Angelique, and she's studying Grayson with narrowed eyes.

"Hey, Angelique," Grayson says. "Congratulations on the little guy."

"Thanks," she says and smiles down at Augustus.

"Listen," Grayson says. "If you've got Angelique here I'm going to run down and tell Sir Drew I'll be up here again today. I don't know if he checked the buddy list or not."

"The buddy list?"

"Yeah, I'm officially your buddy. Although I think I prefer the term 'knight in shining armor.'" He strikes a cheesy pose and grins.

I'm so doomed. Insisting I drive myself to work so I could avoid Grayson as much as possible has done absolutely nothing to convince my traitorous heart that he's off-limits.

"I'll be back in a minute," Grayson says.

"Hey, wait! You're not supposed to go anywhere alone," I remind him.

"Oh, right. Crap."

"Here"—I jump up and reach into my nun pocket—"take Hot Lips." I hold up my stun gun.

He laughs. "Thanks, but I'll stick with my sword. I'll be right back, I swear. Good to see you, Angelique." He gives us a wave and takes off.

"Wow," Angelique says.

"Wow, what?"

"You got it bad."

"What are you talking about?" I ask, avoiding her gaze. She's looking at me with that intense stare she uses to decipher the tourists' innermost truths.

"Is he the guy? The unattainable guy you're in

love with, or is he someone new?"

"What? No. Grayson has a girlfriend. Bree Blair? She plays Catherine Howard?"

"Uh-huh. That doesn't answer my question."

"We go to high school together, and he was there after I found Sarah. He's been trying to help me find the body, since no one else believes me that she's dead. We were looking for Sarah when we found Floyd. He told Hank he'd keep an eye on me. That's probably why Hank assigned him to be my buddy." I stop babbling and sneak a peek at Angelique's face.

She's gone very pale.

"Are you okay?" I ask, suddenly alarmed. "Are you sure you should be out and about so soon? You just had a baby."

"Be very careful, Jules," she says.

"What do you mean?"

"I'm not sure Grayson is someone you should be alone with."

"Don't worry, I know he has a girlfriend. I would never go after someone else's boyfriend. Especially Bree Blair's boyfriend. There's no way I'd have a chance in hell with him anyway."

"I'm not talking about stealing boyfriends, Jules. You said the police are sure that Sarah had an accomplice, right? How did you know where to look for Floyd?"

"We weren't looking for Floyd. We were looking for Sarah. Floyd's the one who told us to look in the iron maiden."

"Did you tell Grayson that?"

"Well, yeah, of course I did."

Angelique grabs my hand. "Jules, promise me you won't go anywhere alone with him."

"Whoa. You're freaking me out here."

"How long have Grayson and Bree been together?"

"For, like, ever. Since sixth grade when he moved to Lunevale and got assigned the seat next to her in homeroom."

"And has he ever given you the time of day before?"

"What? What do you mean?" I don't know where this conversation is going, but I'm starting to get the same feeling you get in a scary movie when the ominous music starts to play.

"I mean, were you friends with Grayson before you took the job here? Before you found Sarah's body?"

"No. I was friends with Bree. Well, it's not like we still hang out all the time, but she's always really nice to me. Grayson just sort of..."

"Just sort of what?"

"Seemed to avoid me. Like everyone else who wasn't busy making fun of me."

"But now?"

"But now...he's my buddy," I say and I can hear how stupid it sounds. "But I swear it's just because of the murders." Oh God. Why do I feel so guilty all of a sudden? And *scared*?

"That's what I'm afraid of," Angelique says. "I told you I already knew about the secret passageway behind the suit of armor because I'd seen someone coming out of the entrance and into the hall, right?"

"Right." And the ominous music builds.

"But I didn't tell you who that person was."

"Who was it?" I ask, even though I know I don't want to know.

"Bree Blair."

Chapter Twenty-Eight
I Know Where the Body Is

Grayson comes back dressed in his squire tunic and I'm completely mortified when Angelique stands up and gets in his face.

"I'm onto your girlfriend, *buddy*," she says. "And I'm letting you know that if anything happens to Jules here, I'm coming for you myself."

"What are you talking about?" Grayson looks totally bewildered.

Augustus starts bawling.

"I'm going to go feed my baby, and then I'm going to have a word with the police. So don't get any ideas, Prince Charming." She turns back to me. "Remember what I said, Jules." Then she blows out the door, Augustus's wails trailing behind her.

"What was that all about?" Grayson asks.

"Why are you being so nice to me all of a sudden, Grayson?" I'm furious with Angelique for holding out on me and furious with myself for actually believing, I'll admit it, that Grayson liked me. As in, *liked* me, liked me.

"What? You're mad at me for being *nice* to you?"

"Before I found Sarah's body, you wouldn't give me the time of day. It was almost like you avoided me *on purpose*. And now you're offering me rides to work and you even get yourself *assigned* as my buddy."

"I didn't get myself assigned. I don't understand why you're so angry."

"I'm not angry. I'm finally realizing how weird it is that you suddenly want to be my friend. Me, Jules Verity, crazy psychic freak." God, I'm so stupid.

"Jules, you're not a freak."

"No? Then what do you call it? And why do you even care?" I just want him to go away. I don't even want to try to figure out what it all means.

"Of course I care. I've been trying to help you, Jules. I'm sorry if I was an ass to you before, it's just..."

"Just what?"

He runs his fingers through his hair and frowns. "I...I need to talk to Bree."

"I bet you do." I'm *afraid* to figure out what it all means.

He looks at me like I'm standing at the edge of the Cliffs of Insanity, getting ready to jump.

"Who's her buddy now that Sarah's not available? And where was she when I got hit by that car?" I ask him, and then the pain and confusion are too much and I let out a sob.

"You're not making any sense. Maybe we should have this conversation later. When you're not so upset."

"Good idea, because there's no way I'm staying in here with you." I jump up and run for the door, tears streaming down my face.

Grayson grabs my arm. "Jules, please. Why are you so angry with me?"

"Let me go. Please don't make me use my stun gun on you."

He drops my arm.

"Angelique saw her, Grayson."

"Saw who? I don't understand any of this."

"She saw Bree. Coming out of the alcove. Bree was in the secret passageway."

Grayson's eyes widen, and he backs away from me. "What are you saying?"

"I don't know. I don't even *want* to know."

"You think Bree had something to do with the murders?" I watch as his expression shifts from horrified to incredulous. "That's ridiculous."

"Is it? No more ridiculous than you suddenly discovering that I exist."

"Jules." He grabs my arm again. "Let's go find Bree. We need to talk about this."

I pull my arm away. "I'm not going anywhere with you, Grayson. Not ever."

As I stumble through the door I hear him whisper, "As you wish."

I make for the stairs, tears blinding me. I run
through the main hallway, determined to get out,
to get away from all the secrets and the lies and the
stupid butterflies. I grab my backpack out of my
cubby in the Great Wardrobe, duck into a dressing
room, and strip off my Maid of Kent costume. I put
on my street clothes and wad my costume up in a ball.
When I throw the curtain open Geoffrey is standing
right outside.

He's holding his enormous pair of scissors by
his side and I notice a dark splotch on his absurd
pumpkin-shaped pants.

"What are you doing?" he asks, looking down at
the crumpled costume.

"I...I have to leave early," I say. "I'm sorry I
wrinkled my costume." I hold the ball of fabric out to
him. "I just...I'm in a hurry."

"What's the matter, Mistress Verity? You seem
awfully upset." Geoffrey takes the costume from
me and tucks it under his arm. Instead of his usual
pristine white jacket he's wearing black velvet.

"It's just...it's too much right now. With finding
Sarah and then Floyd and the police thinking—"

"What do the police think?"

"The police think I had something to do with all
of it, which is ridiculous. But Angelique saw—" I stop
myself before I permanently besmirch Bree's golden
name.

"What did Angelique see?"

"Never mind. I have to go. Thanks, Geoffrey,
but I don't really want to talk about it." I take a step

forward but instead of backing up, Geoffrey leans
into me.

"Someone else saw Sarah's body," he whispers.

"What?" I want him out of my space. I haven't
even processed what just happened with Grayson; I
can't handle any more right now.

"I saw her come out of the secret entrance."

"Who? You saw someone come out of the alcove?
But that's impossible. I was in the hallway and then—"

"Not the alcove, she came out of the other
entrance."

"What entrance? The dungeon or upstairs?" I
can't seem to follow what he's saying.

"The dungeon. And I know where the body is."

Chapter Twenty-Nine
Your Secret's Safe with Me

"Come on, I'll show you," Geoffrey says.

I look around the costume shop and realize there's no one else around. "Um, where's your buddy, Geoffrey? Aren't you supposed to have a buddy?"

"Don't you want to see the body? Come on, let's go."

"To the dungeon? Um, no thanks, I'll pass. Why don't you tell the police what you know?"

"No, not the dungeon, the suit of armor."

"What?" My brain is still scrambling to keep up.

"The suit of armor. It's so ridiculously obvious."

"The body's in the suit of armor? That doesn't make any sense. How would—"

Geoffrey pulls my arm and leads me into the

hallway. "Let's go, before I change my mind."

I follow him down the hallway, and he stops in front of the suit of armor and beckons me forward. "Quick, before someone else comes. Flip open the visor."

"What? Geoffrey, this is crazy. She's been dead for at least three days. Wouldn't someone have smelled her by now if she was in the suit of armor?"

"Well then, flip open the visor and see. The front part of the headpiece, pull it up so you can see inside."

He points at the helmet with his scissors, and even though I know it's ridiculous and there's no way Sarah's body is inside the suit, I'm suddenly deeply afraid of opening the helmet.

I step forward. I reach one hand up, and Geoffrey shoves me from behind, and we're spinning. The secret entrance slides open and I'm back in the passageway, Geoffrey sandwiching me between him and the suit of armor. I scream but it's too late; the entrance is already resealed. Geoffrey pulls his scissors out of the armored hand and I realize he must have used them to trigger the mechanism in the absence of the ax. He sticks the pointed tip of the scissors under my chin.

"Don't bother screaming again. The walls are three feet thick." He pushes something into my hands. "You can hold this. I'm going to need my hands free," he says, and I realize he's handed me my balled-up nun costume.

I'm about to drop it when I remember the stun gun. I never took it out of the hidden pocket.

"You saw the blood on my trunk hose, didn't you? Who would have thought the old man to have so much blood in him, eh? But they're silk. I couldn't just wash them in the sink—it would destroy the fabric. And I didn't think anyone would notice, a red stain on red pants. But you, you already knew, didn't you?" His body is still pressed up against me, and he sprays my cheek with flecks of spittle as he talks.

"Geoffrey, I don't know what you're talking about." I wince as the scissors bite into my skin.

"'Be soft and attend thy soiled slops!' Isn't that what you told me, Miss Know-It-All? Well you *don't* know it all, do you?" He pushes me forward. "Do you still want to find Sarah? Floyd gave you the answer, you just didn't look hard enough. And the police must not have taken you very seriously, because they didn't either." He pushes me down the passageway toward the steps to the dungeon. "I was going to be the next Walter Plunkett, you know."

"Um, who's Walter Plunkett?" I ask, hoping it's a long story.

We reach the stairs, and he pulls me tight against him so we can go down the steps together. "*Gone with the Wind? Singin' in the Rain? Little Women?* And more than a hundred and fifty other movies? How can you not know Walter Plunkett? He was a genius. His costumes were meticulously researched and flawlessly accurate. Converse sneakers for Marie Antoinette? Mixing Degas with a ruff? He would never have done anything so ridiculous! He had too much class. And so do I. I'm the foremost authority on period costumes! If someone wanted historical accuracy they came to me! But then that little hussy cuddled up to the director and suddenly I was out of a job. I worked for years to establish my reputation, and all she had to do was shake her ass. And Sarah was the same."

"Sarah was sleeping with Hank?" I say, totally shocked at the idea.

"She had him under her spell all right. She was stealing things from right under his nose. The fabric I could maybe have forgiven. Replacing my gorgeous silks with polyester linings? I understand the lust for a Scalamandré silk damask, but substituting fake jewels for the real ones I'd so meticulously sewn on? Can you imagine if we had sent King Henry's Whitehall ensemble to the British Museum that way? They would have laughed it right out of the building. And she was destroying his beautiful necklaces and jeweled weapons. That lovely little dagger I used to kill Floyd. It was unacceptable. And when I confronted her she said it didn't even matter. That no one cared if the gowns were made of silk or polyester. Polyester! Can you imagine? She actually laughed in my face. 'What are you going to do about it, Geoffrey? You're just a washed-up has-been working in a cheesy dinner theater in the middle of Looneytown.'"

We reach the bottom step, and he spins me around. "The things I make are beautiful. No one else can re-create history through fabric like I do. No one. The British Museum wants my garments! The

British Museum!" His face is inches from my own, but he's practically screaming at me, as if he needs to make sure I hear the importance of what he's saying.

"I've never seen costumes as beautiful as the ones here at Tudor Times," I say, truthfully. "They take my breath away. Sarah obviously didn't understand."
So you took her breath away.

"No, she didn't. And Floyd, he was not a nice man. He was a snoop, like you. He found out what Sarah was doing and blackmailed her. She gave him a share of the jewels, and he not only kept quiet about it, he started helping her get into the castle at night."

Geoffrey pulls me with him and feels along the stone wall until he triggers the opening leading to the dungeon. We step through the wooden cabinet. In the corner of the dungeon stands the iron maiden surrounded by the detritus of the *CSI* team, but there are no police here now.

"They're all upstairs conducting interviews," Geoffrey says, as if reading my mind. "Floyd was right, I used the iron maiden, but I didn't simply hide Sarah inside. There's an extra secret not even the police figured out. Why don't you open her dress and I'll demonstrate?"

"Um, no thanks. I'm happy to take your word for it, Geoffrey. Can we go back upstairs now? It's a little chilly down here." I take a step toward the door, and he yanks me back.

He reaches out and pulls the handle to open the iron maiden. "Get in there. Now." He gives me a push and I stumble forward. "Floyd told me the secret when

I was working on an Elizabethan gown King Henry commissioned for a new banquet performance. The ruff reminded Floyd of the iron maiden. Of course he called it a collar, not a ruff. Imbecile. He should know better. Oh yes, Floyd told me lots of secrets. I was going to hide his body, too, but the mechanism was stuck and I didn't have a chance to get rid of him before you came snooping around again."

I yelp as he nicks me with the scissors. I feel a warm trickle of blood run down my neck. "Don't do this, Geoffrey," I say. "Let's go back upstairs. I'll help you explain to King Henry what was going on."

"Floyd came down here looking for Sarah. And I wanted to help him find her. Just like I'm going to help you. I know you won't stop snooping until you find her. Would you like to know where she is?"

I'm not sure how to answer this question safely, and I'm too busy trying to get the cap off the stun gun inside my balled-up costume, so I don't say anything.

"Floyd knew I was the only one he told the iron maiden's secret to. I had to kill him or he was going to tell."

"I'm not going to tell anyone, Geoffrey. All I wanted to do was prove that I'm not crazy. That's it. I wasn't trying to catch Sarah's killer, I just wanted to show everyone that I didn't hallucinate a dead body. But listen. Everyone still thinks I'm crazy! They think I'm Sarah's accomplice. They're not going to believe anything I say. Your secret's safe with me. Now can we just—"

"No," Geoffrey says and he shoves me into the

iron maiden. "You want to find the body? I'll show you where she is," he shrieks. As he reaches up with one hand toward the disintegrating face of the iron maiden, he raises the hand holding the scissors as if preparing to plunge them into my chest. I take advantage of the fact that the scissors are no longer at my throat and pull the cap off the stun gun and thrust it forward into Geoffrey's chest. His eyes open wide as I push the button, then his arm jerks and he drops the scissors, but it's too late.

Chapter Thirty

Mystery Solved

The metal floor of the iron maiden gives way beneath me, and I drop through a gaping hole. I brace for impact, but instead I land with a splash and find myself completely under water. My feet hit something solid and I push off, breaking the surface with a sputter and a cough. The water is cold and deep enough that I can no longer touch bottom. I look up. Geoffrey's head appears silhouetted in the circular trapdoor hidden beneath the iron maiden.

"Well, mystery solved!" Geoffrey yells down at me. "Now you know where the body went. Too bad no one else will ever know."

"Help! Geoffrey, I can't swim!" I yell and the water closes over my head again. I push with my arms and bob back up. "Geoffrey, help!" I yell again and then let myself sink, holding my breath for as long as I can. Desperate for air, I return to the surface to find the trapdoor closed and Geoffrey gone.

I take in great gulps of air, trying not to notice the smell assaulting my nostrils, knowing what it must mean.

Dim light filters in from somewhere above me. I'm still holding my stun gun/flashlight and I press the flashlight button, hoping against hope that it will still work despite the repeated dunking it's just received. Nothing happens. I try the stun gun button, but the water seems to have killed it as well. Or maybe zapping Geoffrey used up all its power.

I turn in a slow circle. I'm in the center of a rectangular pool surrounded by a collection of white marble statues separated by tall columns. As my eyes adjust to the gloom I see that the walls and ceiling are covered in beautiful blue and gold mosaics. I appear to be in some kind of underground bathhouse featuring a secret entrance hidden in a medieval instrument of torture. The more of wacky Mr. Lune's secrets I discover, the less I'm inclined to like him.

I catch sight of something floating a few feet away from me in a corner of the pool. I know what it is even before I get close enough to see for sure. I've found Sarah, just as Geoffrey promised. She's floating facedown in the water, and there can be no doubt she's dead. I swim to the steps at the other end of the pool and climb out. I put both hands over my mouth as I gag on the realization that I've been floating in water containing a decomposing corpse.

I can't assume that Geoffrey bought my drowning act, and I don't want to be here if he comes back. I can see the outline of the trapdoor in the ceiling, but there's no way to reach it. I quickly case the room and find a switch that brings to life several of the alabaster lamps lining the bathhouse. The light bounces off the tiles and the effect is beautiful: it turns the surface of the water into a shimmering pane of glass, broken only by the body floating silently on the surface. I try to avoid looking at Sarah's corpse, but the smell is inescapable. I need to get out of this place.

I'm jumping up and down, trying to warm myself up and shake off some of the contaminated water saturating my clothing, when I spot a backpack lying next to one of the statues. I rush over to it, remembering Jared's story about Sarah's text message to Geoffrey. According to Jared, her cell phone signal was coming from somewhere inside the castle. I pat the outside pockets and let out a whoop of triumph when I feel a rectangular bulge. I reach my hand inside and pull out something that feels cool and metallic. Breath mints. Oh goodie, at least I'll have something to eat if I'm trapped down here for long. Or maybe I can stuff them up my nose to escape the smell of Sarah's putrefaction. In the other pocket I find a flashlight and a set of keys, but no phone.

I unzip the main compartment and find a carefully folded stack of fabric, as well as a small velvet bag containing a jumble of jewelry pieces, and a wallet with Sarah Buckley's driver's license tucked inside. So not helpful. I throw the backpack down in frustration. And then I see the cell phone lying on the ground to the side of the statue.

"Oh, thank you, thank you, thank you, Sarah!" I grab the phone and push a button. An image of a depleted battery appears. "Come on battery, I just need one call." The screen goes blank. I try pressing and holding the button, then pressing it repeatedly, then shaking the phone with frustration, but the screen remains impassively blank. It might as well be floating in the pool with Sarah—it's clearly just as dead. I shove it in my pocket and grab the flashlight. I'm relieved to discover that it, at least, still works.

I head for the dark hallway halfway down the room where the light from the alabaster lamps doesn't quite reach. There are three doors on each side of the hallway and I try them one by one. Three of them lead to small dressing rooms, and the other three are private bathrooms complete with showers. I consider rinsing myself off but decide I have more pressing priorities. I head back to the pool room and shine my flashlight on the tile ceiling. In between two mosaics featuring naked mermaids are several rows of what look like glass bricks set into the tile. They're letting in a small amount of light, which could either be sunlight from outside or light from a room above. I try to orient myself in the castle. I know there are no glass bricks in the floor of the dungeon, but I'm not sure what else is on this side of the castle. Angelique was too busy playing *CSI* to give me a proper tour.

High up on the wall opposite the trapdoor,

a beautifully tiled diving platform juts over the rectangular pool. I make my way up one of the curving staircases leading to the top of the platform, where I find a set of doors carved with more naked mermaids and assorted sea creatures. I grasp both handles and pull. They're locked. I kick them, slam them with my shoulder, curse them, but they don't budge. My exit options are limited to jumping off the platform into the pool or going back down the stairs. I choose the stairs.

Down at pool level again, I head for the decorative alcove tucked beneath the diving platform. It features a carved marble statue of a naked woman standing on a huge shell.

"It would be really helpful if you had an ax in your hand," I tell her. I'm examining the wall behind her in case she's conveniently hiding another secret entrance when I hear a noise on the platform above me. Someone is unlocking the doors.

The sound of one of the doors scraping open is followed by the *thud* of footsteps. I flatten myself against the wall. If it's Geoffrey coming back for me, I at least want the element of surprise.

There's silence above me. Then I hear the owner of the footsteps making a *tutt*ing sound and I know it's definitely Geoffrey.

"Now, now, Mistress Verity. Let's not play games. You're not in the pool with Sarah, so I know you're here somewhere. There's no other way out."

Shit. I would kill for that ax right about now.

"I came down to collect a few things from Sarah's

backpack to plant in your van." He starts down the stairs to my right, the sound of his footsteps reverberating off the tile walls. "And instead I find you inconveniently alive." He's standing at the bottom of the stairs now.

I'm tucked behind the statue, praying he can't hear the sound of my heart slamming against my ribs.

He turns slowly and smiles at me. "There you are." His wickedly sharp-looking scissors are in his right hand, and he's wearing one of the dining room smocks over his costume.

I touch the place on my neck where he cut me earlier and wince at the pain.

"I should have known your drowning scene was overly theatrical. You've obviously never watched someone drown. Contrary to popular belief, there's no dramatic splashing or screaming for help. They simply sink below the surface and fail to return. At least that's how it happened with my former assistant on *Little Minks*. She was at a party at the director's house and for some reason she decided to jump into the pool even though she couldn't swim. Unfortunately, no one was there to save her."

I shiver involuntarily. Sarah wasn't the first person Geoffrey murdered. But I'm really hoping Floyd will be the last.

He cocks his head to the side. "You're the one who tipped me off to what Sarah was doing, you know."

"Me? I didn't even know her."

"It was your comment about cabbage that inspired me to follow her on the night she died."

"Cabbage?" While Geoffrey is doing his looney-tunes routine I'm desperately looking for a way to escape. If I lunge for the other set of stairs I might be able to make it.

"Yes, you said, 'The cabbage is only the beginning,' and you were right." Geoffrey is waving the scissors around as he talks. "Tudor tailors called scraps of cloth 'cabbage.' Sarah started out by stealing pieces of fabric and trim to use in her online shop and worked her way up to King Henry's jewels. I caught her in the act and strangled her with one of the necklaces she defaced. You, however, are proving particularly difficult to dispose of, Mistress Verity. If you'd had the decency to die, or at least end up in the hospital when I ran you off the road, I wouldn't have had to kill Floyd, you know."

If there was any doubt before, I am now certain that Geoffrey is completely gaga. "So it's my fault Floyd's dead?"

"To be fair, I would say it's Floyd's fault, but you certainly contributed. Now why don't you come over here and we'll deal with this once and for all?"

"It's too late," I say.

"Pardon?" He takes a step toward me.

I pull out Sarah's phone and hold it up. "I called the police. You left Sarah's phone down here, Geoffrey. I called 911 and told them where I am and what you did. They'll be here any second."

He laughs. "I hardly think so, Mistress Verity.

When I brought Sarah's things down I discovered there's no service in this room. I had to take her phone upstairs to send myself a text from her."

Shit. I throw the phone at him and make a break for the stairs. I slip on the wet tile and fall to my knees.

Geoffrey hauls me up and puts me in a chokehold with the point of the scissors pressed against my back. "I don't want to have to get bloodstains out of another jacket, so I'd prefer to strangle you. But if you try to get away again, I *will* use these."

I feel the scissors pierce through the fabric of my shirt and into my skin, and I cry out in pain.

"That's enough, Geoffrey," a voice bellows from above.

Geoffrey drags me backward and I look up to see Hank standing on the platform at the top of the stairs. I'm filled with equal parts awe and immense relief, seeing him looming above us looking like a fiery-haired avenging angel.

"Your Majesty, what are you doing here?" Geoffrey sounds like a little kid who's been caught misbehaving.

"Let her go, Geoffrey."

"I can't do that, Your Majesty." Geoffrey tightens the arm around my neck and points the scissors at Hank.

"Put down the scissors. You don't want to fight me."

"Your Majesty, you don't understand." He's gesticulating with the scissors as he speaks, and I try to shake some of the water off my hands so I can make a grab for them, but his agitated movements are making it difficult to keep my balance.

"I believe I do, Geoffrey. You killed Sarah and Floyd, and you intended to kill Mistress Verity as well."

"I didn't mean to kill Sarah. But she made a mockery of us both and I lost my temper. Surely you can understand that, Your Majesty?"

"I'm afraid I can't. I need you to come with me now or I will be forced to do something unpleasant." King Henry draws his sword.

Geoffrey moans and points the scissors at my neck.

In the silence that follows I hear the soft patter of water droplets falling from my sodden clothes onto the tile floor, then the rustling of silk as Hank takes a step toward the stairs. Inside my panicked brain, a memory flutters its wings.

I look up at Hank. "King Henry?"

"Yes, Mistress Verity? Are you all right?"

"I've been better. But listen, are you wearing your Whitehall outfit? The one that's supposed to go to the British Museum?"

Hank looks down at the jewel-studded doublet he's wearing. "Indeed, I am."

"I bet it's made from some of that really expensive silk fabric, right, Geoffrey?"

"Of course it is. Only the best for His Majesty."

"Water stains are mightier than the sword!" I call up to Hank, hoping he gets it.

Hank drops his sword with a deafening *clang* and starts unbuttoning his doublet.

"What are you doing? Why are you taking that off?" Geoffrey demands.

"Let her go." Hank releases the final button. "Or the doublet goes in the water."

"You wouldn't do that." Geoffrey's arm tightens around my neck. "That doublet represents the finest work I've ever done."

"I know it does, Geoffrey." Hanks slips the doublet off and steps forward.

"It's been promised to the British Museum. No, Your Majesty! The water will ruin the silk. Stop, please!"

Geoffrey is squeezing my neck so tightly I can't breathe. Black spots appear at edges of my vision.

Hank throws the doublet.

Geoffrey screams, drops his scissors, and dives after the falling doublet.

I grab the scissors and sprint for the stairs. When I get to the top, I join Hank at the edge of the platform. We look down at the pool where Geoffrey is clutching the sodden doublet and sobbing as he flounders in the water.

"Do you think he can swim?" Hank asks.

"I think so," I say. "Sorry about the doublet."

"That is the least of my concerns, Mistress Verity."

I turn away from the pool and its ruined inhabitants. "How'd you know where to find me?"

"Mr. Chandler came to me and told me you were missing. We were scouring the castle for you when I remembered your banquet performance. 'Mermaids blush when clothes unmake the man.'" He points at the ceiling. "As far as I know, this room contains the only mermaids in Lunewood Castle."

"Seriously? Wow."

"I believe your butterflies are in effect, Mistress Verity." He looks down at Geoffrey, still sobbing in the pool. "I fear your second prophecy will also prove to be true: 'No amount of bathing will ever make him clean.'"

Chapter Thirty-One
Just to be Clear

*H*ank stays in the bathhouse to guard Geoffrey while I run upstairs to find the police. On the way back down I explain to Officer Kilbride about Sarah and Floyd and even Geoffrey's former assistant on *Little Minks*.

"How did Mr. Bacon know where to find you?" he asks.

"He figured out one of my prophecies."

"I see. So you do have a gift after all?"

"Yeah. I still don't really understand it, but it's hard to deny something that probably just saved my life."

"You're a very lucky lady, Miss Verity." He stops and puts a hand on my arm. "Are you ever going to tell me what you were hiding?"

"It's not important," I say and pull away from him. "It had nothing to do with the murders. It was about a boy."

"Grayson Chandler?"

I stop walking. "Yeah. How did you know? Don't tell me you're psychic, too?"

"Hardly. I just finished having a long talk with Bree Blair. She told me she knew about the passageway."

"She did?"

"Yes. You might be interested in what else she has to say." He gives me a disarming smile and keeps walking. "But right now I'd like to see this body before it disappears again."

The police take Geoffrey into custody without incident, although he refuses to let go of King Henry's doublet. I find some dry clothes to change into in the Great Wardrobe and spend at least half an hour in one of bathroom showers trying to scrub away the gruesome taint of the bathhouse pool. Hank and I meet Officer Kilbride in the study and he asks us endless questions about Sarah and Floyd and Geoffrey.

Despite Officer Lasky's ridiculous theory—which was really just an attempt to scare me into confessing whatever sinister thing they thought I was hiding—there was no accomplice. Sarah was acting on her own, stealing fabric and jewels from the Great Wardrobe and incorporating them into items for sale in her online shop. I tell Officer Kilbride what Geoffrey told me about Floyd blackmailing Sarah for a share of the jewels, and he tells us that Mike the Knight confessed that Sarah asked him to help her replace the jewels in some of King Henry's weapons. Mike knew what she was up to, but refused to help her. He claimed he was planning to turn her in but when she went missing he was afraid of being implicated.

Finally Officer Kilbride tells me I'm free to go. "But I'll be in touch, Miss Verity. Oh, and one more thing. You were right about the ketchup."

"I was?"

"Yes. Suffice it to say, there's a woman who's alive today and getting the help she needs, because of you."

"Because of *ketchup*?"

"Because of *you*. You can read about it in the *Lunevale Gazette* tomorrow. In the meantime, I think you have someone else to talk to."

I nod and open the door.

"Mistress Verity, I'd say you've earned at least a week off, with pay," Hank says. "I do hope you'll be back?"

"Thanks, Your Majesty. That's really generous of you. I'm not sure what I'm going to do. But I'll let you know as soon as I figure it out," I say, and close the door behind me.

Bree is sitting in the hallway outside the door and she jumps up when she sees me. "Jules, I need to talk to you." She puts a hand on my arm.

I pull my arm away and keep walking. "I'm a little talked out right now. Did you hear about Geoffrey? He's been arrested for killing Sarah. And Floyd."

"I know. And I know Angelique told you she saw me come out of the secret entrance to the passageway on the night Sarah died. Jules, I had nothing to do with Sarah's murder. I told the police everything."

"Yeah, that's what Officer Kilbride said. I'm sorry, Bree, but can we talk about this later? I really just want to go home right now. The last few hours have kind of been hell and—"

"Grayson and I broke up."

This stops me in my tracks. "What?"

She reaches out and takes my hand. "Come on, let's go find a quiet place to talk."

"You're not going to lead me to some secret room and try to kill me, are you?"

"Nope. I was going to suggest the garden. I figured you could use a little sunshine."

We walk outside and find a bench just inside the hedge maze. Bree turns to face me.

"I want you to know the truth. You have been through hell, Jules, and I'm really sorry." She looks down at her lap. "This is ridiculously hard for me. You're the first friend I've told besides Grayson. But you need to know the truth." She meets my eyes again. "I was in the passageway the night Sarah died, but I had nothing to do with her murder. I went in there to meet someone. We...we wanted a place where we'd have some privacy, somewhere we could be alone. And when we heard someone else enter the passageway from upstairs, we got scared and I came out the entrance behind the suit of armor. I never even saw Sarah." She stops and takes my hand. "The person I was with? It wasn't Grayson."

My eyes must be bugging out, because Bree says, "I know. Jules, the person I was with was Kaitlyn."

"Your *lady-in-waiting*?"

"Yes. And just so you know, she didn't see Sarah, either. She left through the entrance in the dungeon so we wouldn't be seen leaving the passageway together."

"Oh."

"I was definitely hiding something, but it had nothing to do with Sarah's murder, I swear."

I'm pretty sure I understand what she's saying, but I want to be sure. "So you're...?"

"I'm in love with Kaitlyn. Not Grayson."

"I so did not see that coming."

"I know. Everyone thinks I have this perfect life and the perfect boyfriend, but it's a lie. Grayson is my best friend, but he hasn't been my boyfriend for a long time. Not since I realized I had a crush on one of my girlfriends in seventh grade. I was madly in love with her for years but I knew she didn't feel the same way, so there didn't seem to be any point in telling anyone how I felt. Grayson knew, of course, but no one else. I didn't want to risk losing my friends if they found out the truth. Everyone assumed that Grayson and I were more than friends, and neither of us did anything to correct their assumptions.

"But then I met Kaitlyn and I wanted to be with

her and I didn't know what to do, and then Floyd told me about the passageways and we started meeting there, just to talk and be alone without worrying about what everyone else thought. I knew I was going to have to tell Grayson eventually, but it was all happening so fast and I didn't want him to be embarrassed. To have everyone think he'd been dumped by his girlfriend because she'd realized she was a lesbian. It wasn't like that, but no one else knew that. And then today when he told me that you knew I'd been in the passageway, I was horrified that anyone would think I had anything to do with Sarah's death, and I knew that the only possible way to fix everything was to tell the truth.

"And then when Grayson and I were talking, I realized he had feelings for someone else, too, and it all suddenly made sense. *He* was afraid to tell *me*. Isn't that ridiculous?" She busts into a gigantic grin at this, but I feel strangely numb. All I can think is, *Who is Grayson in love with? And what if it's not me? What if he's finally free and he's already found someone else?*

Bree tilts her head and tries to get a better look at my face. "Are you okay, Jules?" And suddenly she looks like she's going to cry.

I realize she must think I'm upset about her revelation instead of petrified at the thought that Grayson might already have another Bree.

"If you don't want to be my friend I totally—"

I throw my arms around her. "Bree, of course I want to be your friend. You're the only person besides

Cami who never seems to care what a freak I am."

"You're not a freak, Jules. You're amazing. And anyway, normal is overrated."

I let go of her and we lean back to look at each other.

"God, I'm so glad that's over with," Bree says, giving me her Miss America smile. "Are you sure you're okay?"

"I can't tell you how relieved I am that you're not a murderer." I manage to give her a genuine grin. "And I think Kaitlyn is enormously lucky, because you're one of the best people I know. And I'll do whatever I can to make things easier for you at school or work or whatever. I'm really sorry that I thought you were in any way involved in Sarah's death." I feel my face start to crumple again. "But I'm kind of a mess right now, so if you don't mind, I'm going to go home and try not to think about Tudor Times for at least a week."

"Oh, God. I'm so sorry. You've been through hell and here I am going on and on about my problems. Go find Grayson, he'll give you a ride home."

"I've got my mom's van. And I don't really think Grayson wants to talk to me right now." Not after the things I said to him in the Oratory.

"Jules. Go find Grayson." She gives me another hug and then whispers in my ear, "It was you, by the way."

"Wait, what? What was me?" I ask, but she's already running down the path away from me.

I'm still sitting there trying to figure it out when

Grayson appears in all his romance-cover glory.

"Hey, Buttercup," he says, giving me an awkward wave.

"Hey," I say, and wish the numb feeling would come back.

"Bree said you were over here."

"Yup." Just sitting here about to ugly-cry over this guy I'm in love with who probably already has another girlfriend.

"That's some dress. Where's the nun habit?"

"I thought I'd try the princess look for a change." When I was picking out dry clothes in the Great Wardrobe I happened to find a sumptuous Tudor gown that gave me fabulous cleavage. Well, as fabulous as mine gets, anyway.

"Oh, so it's Princess Buttercup now? Do you mind if I sit down?"

"No, go ahead." Oh God. I like him so much my heart feels like it's going to explode right out of my minimal cleavage.

"You found Sarah."

"Yeah. Turns out she really was dead."

"I believed you, you know."

I don't know how to respond.

"Are you okay, Jules?"

"No, not really." *I will not ugly-cry in front of Grayson. I will not ugly-cry in front of Grayson.*

Grayson takes a deep breath. "Bree said she told you about Kaitlyn."

"Yeah, she did."

Our eyes lock, and I have to look away. My heart

feels like a calving glacier, pieces of it breaking off and sliding away. Because there's no way he's in love with me, Jules Verity, the freak with the blurting disorder.

"Can I tell you a story?"

"Uh, sure."

"I have this friend. When he was in sixth grade his family moved to a new town and he found himself assigned a desk next to the most beautiful girl he'd ever met and he was instantly smitten. He told her he wanted to marry her and she agreed to let him be in love with her. They became best friends and he constantly hoped that someday she would fall madly in love with him, but though she *loved* him, she wasn't *in love* with him and the boy decided that, for the time being, that was enough.

"Then one day this girl told the boy that she now knew she could never be his one true love, that she was in love with someone else. The boy's heart was broken. But then the girl confessed that she knew that this new love would never be able to be more than a friend to her. It was a vicious irony and they both were very sad. But they decided to stay best friends and everyone else assumed that they were also dating.

"And the girl continued to love her impossible love from afar and one day the boy found himself falling in love with this impossible love as well. And he too knew he could never be with this impossible love because it would break his best friend's heart. And so he loved this new love from afar, too.

"And eventually, the girl grew tired of despairing over unrequited love and decided she would find a love that wasn't so impossible. But the boy continued to love the impossible new love from afar. Until one day he discovered that the impossible might actually be possible."

"Um, Grayson? That's a nice story, but why are you telling me all this?"

"I just...I wanted to explain. I was hoping... Did she tell you it was you?"

"What?" My heart is suddenly booming.

"I lied. That story wasn't about my friend. The girl Bree was in love with? She was constantly talking about her and how smart and beautiful and funny she was, and at first it was annoying because I wanted her to be in love with me, but somewhere along the way I realized she was right. And then I was completely torn, because how horrible would it be to break up with your faux girlfriend because you were in love with the girl she was in love with and could never be with? I couldn't do that to Bree. And then when you thought she had something to do with the murders she freaked out and—"

"Stop! What did you just say?"

"That Bree didn't have anything to do with the murders?"

"No, the part before that. *What* was me?" My heart is beating so fast I think I might be having a heart attack, and I can't die without knowing the answer to this question.

"The girl Bree was in love with before Kaitlyn? It

was you, Jules."

Brain officially blown. How could someone as perfect as Bree Blair be in love with *me*? Wait. If Bree was in love with me that means... Suddenly I'm convinced I'm not having a heart attack, I'm having a brain aneurysm. Because if Grayson was in love with the girl Bree was in love with... Except there's no way the two most perfect people in the world could be in love with me. Smart, beautiful, and funny? *Me?* "Uh, I'm really, really confused," I finally say.

"I should warn you that communication apparently isn't my strong suit."

"Yeah. You're talking to the girl with the involuntary blurting disorder. I think I win the awkward communication award. So, um, that was a great story, but, just so we're clear, this new love you were talking about? What's her name?"

Grayson smiles that dimpled smile that makes my heart feel like it's going to Zumba right out of my chest. "Juliet."

I gulp. It's really hard to think clearly with an exploded brain. "Oh. And um, just to make it perfectly, absolutely, 100 percent clear, what's her last name?"

"Verity."

"And, um, where does she live?"

"Lunevale, California."

"So, again, in the interest of clarity, you *were* in love with this impossible new love, or you still are?"

"I still am. Except..."

"Except *what*?"

"It turns out it's not so impossible." He leans closer. "Jules, I—"

"No, wait!" I hold my hand up, and Grayson looks like I've just zapped him with my Hot Lips stun gun. "I have to tell you something. I'm a terrible person. I *wanted* to think those horrible things about Bree because she's always seemed so unattainably perfect and for as long as I can remember I've been madly in love with her boyfriend." I pause. "Who, it turns out, is not her boyfriend."

"Wait. What?" Grayson says.

"Never mind. I just wanted to apologize. I was so completely wrong it isn't even funny."

"You're madly in love with Bree Blair's boyfriend?"

"Ex-boyfriend. Or...best friend. I don't know, it's all very confusing. All I know is he makes my heart feel like it's going to explode out of my chest and he probably thinks I'm the biggest moron in the world and there's no way I'd ever have a chance with him even if I hadn't accused his girlfriend of murder. Ex-girlfriend. Best friend. Whatever."

"Let's make this absolutely clear, because I want to make sure I know exactly what we're talking about right now. This guy you mentioned, what's his name?"

My mouth goes dry. "Grayson Chandler," I whisper.

"I was hoping you'd say that," he says, and leans toward me.

My heart is screaming, *Kiss him! Kiss him! KISS HIM!!* and my head is screaming, *No way! No way! NO WAY!!* and I have no idea what to do next so of course I blurt something ridiculous. "Where do the noses go?"

Grayson laughs, and those abs, those abs I've been dreaming about for *years*, are so close I could just reach out and touch them, and then I notice his lips are even closer and he's kissing me and oh, wow, it's a million times better than I'd ever imagined it would be. Somehow I've gone from a lovesick nun searching for a dead body in a dungeon to a princess kissing her knight in shining armor in a castle garden. Okay, maybe he's only a squight, but still. It's *Grayson Chandler* and he's kissing me. Me, Jules Verity, who might not be so cursed after all.

"Wow," Grayson says when we finally stop kissing.

"We're much better at that than the whole talking thing," I say.

"Definitely. But I still think we should work on both."

"Definitely," I say. "And we should probably get to work right away. Lost time and all that." And I kiss him again.

Acknowledgments

I'm indebted to a number of marvelous people for making all the words that came before these possible. My agent, Kathleen Rushall, who, as Gran would say, is the bomb-diggity. My editor, Alycia Tornetta, for getting my story (and my sense of humor), and the entire crew at Entangled Teen for being my champions. Ellen Hopkins and Suzanne Morgan Williams, who are responsible for bringing my fairy godmentor, Emma Dryden, and the whole Mentish tribe, into my life through the incomparable Nevada SCBWI Mentor Program. The Splinters, for knowing when to hold my hand and when to kick my butt, and doing both. My sistren: Amy Allgeyer, Donna Cooner, Julie Dillard, Sue Fliess, Beth Hull, Katherine Longshore (who gets a special shout-out for all things Tudor), Sarah McGuire, Hazel Mitchell, Heather Petty, Veronica Rossi, and Talia Vance for being genius writers, readers and friends. LYLP! My sister, Corinne, for being a rock when I need one, and for loving books as much as I do. My mom, Donna, to whom I owe so much more than 10 percent. My dad, Bill, whose prose is purple on purpose, for imparting a profound passion for playing with words. And lastly, to Dan and the L's, who believe in magic, and me.

About the Author

K.C. Held was born and raised in California with stopovers in Honduras, Mexico, and France. Married to her high school sweetheart, and mom to two avid bookworms, she holds an MFA in costume design and has worked as a freelance costumer in opera, theater, film, and television. Although she once spent a summer working in a castle, there were no dead bodies involved.

www.kcheld.com

GRAB THE ENTANGLED TEEN
RELEASES READERS ARE
TALKING ABOUT!

FORGET TOMORROW
BY PINTIP DUNN

It's Callie's seventeenth birthday and, like everyone else, she's eagerly awaiting her vision—a memory sent back in time to sculpt each citizen into the person they're meant to be. Only in her vision, she sees herself murdering her gifted younger sister. Before she can process what it means, Callie is arrested. With the help of her childhood crush, Logan, she escapes the hellish prison called Limbo. But on the run from her future, as well as the government, Callie must figure out how to protect her sister from the biggest threat of all—Callie herself.

NEXIS
BY A.L. DAVROE

A Natural Born amongst genetically-altered Aristocrats, all Ella ever wanted was to be like everyone else. Augmented and perfect. Then...the crash. Devastated by her father's death and struggling with her new physical limitations, Ella is terrified to learn she is not just alone, but little more than a prisoner. Her only escape is to lose herself in Nexis, the hugely popular virtual reality game her father created. In Nexis she meets Guster, who offers Ella guidance, friendship...and something more. But Nexis isn't quite the game everyone thinks it is. And it's been waiting for Ella.

THE BOOK OF IVY
BY AMY ENGEL

What would you kill for?

After a brutal nuclear war, the United States was left decimated. A small group of survivors eventually banded together. My name is Ivy Westfall, and my mission is simple: to kill the president's son—my soon-to-be husband—and return the Westfall family to power. The problem is, Bishop Lattimer isn't the cruel, heartless boy my family warned me to expect. But there is no escape from my fate. Bishop must die. And I must be the one to kill him…

ATLANTIS RISING
BY GLORIA CRAW

Alison McKye isn't exactly human. She's a Child of Atlantis, an ancient race of beings with strange and powerful gifts. She has the ability to "push" thoughts into the minds of others, but her gift also makes her a target. There's a war brewing between the Children of Atlantis, and humans are caught in the middle. If Alison's gift falls into the wrong hands, there's no telling what might happen. But when it comes to protecting those she loves, there's nothing she won't do...

Tarnished
by Kate Jarvik Birch

Genetically engineered "pet" Ella escaped to Canada, but while she can think and act as she pleases, back home, pets are turning up dead. With help from a *very* unexpected source, Ella slips deep into the dangerous black market, posing as a tarnished pet available to buy or sell. If she's lucky, she'll be able to rescue Penn and expose the truth about the breeding program. If she fails, Ella will pay not only with her life, but the lives of everyone she's tried to save...

The Summer Marked
by Rebekah Purdy

Salome Montgomery left humankind behind to be with Gareth in the Kingdom of Summer. But dark forces are rising, her happily-ever-after is coming apart, and the Kingdom is on the brink of war. When she sends a frantic PLEASE HURRY message to her bestie, Kadie Byers is ripped from the human world and pulled into the kingdoms of Faerie, where she's shocked to learn that Salome's monsters are real. Worse, unless she and Salome find a way to survive the deadly chaos, they'll lose themselves to the deadly, icy grasp of an extremely vengeful Winter Queen...

OBLIVION
BY JENNIFER L. ARMENTROUT

The epic love story of *Obsidian* as told by its hero, Daemon Black! I knew the moment Katy Swartz moved in next door, there was going to be trouble. And trouble's the last thing I need, since I'm not exactly from around here. My people arrived on Earth from Lux, a planet thirteen billion light years away. But Kat is getting to me in ways no one else has, and I can't stop myself from wanting her. But falling for Katy—a human—won't just place her in danger. It could get us all killed, and that's one thing I'll never let happen…

THE BODY INSTITUTE
BY CAROL RIGGS

Thanks to cutting-edge technology, Morgan Dey is a top teen Reducer at The Body Institute. She temporarily lives in someone else's body and gets them in shape so they're slimmer and healthier. But there are a few catches. Morgan can never remember anything while in her "Loaner" body, including flirt-texting with the super-cute Reducer she just met or the uneasy feeling that the director of The Body Institute is hiding something. Still, it's all worth it in the name of science. Until the glitches start. Now she'll have to decide if being a Reducer is worth the cost of her body *and* soul…

THIEF of LIES

a Library Jumpers novel

·BRENDA DRAKE·

Read on for a sneak peek!

CHAPTER ONE

Only God and the vendors at Haymarket wake early on Saturday mornings. The bloated clouds spattered rain against my faded red umbrella. I strangled the wobbly handle and dodged shoppers along the tiny makeshift aisle of Boston's famous outdoor produce market. The site, just off the North End, was totally packed and stinky. The fruits and vegetables for sale were rejects from nearby supermarkets—basically, they were cheap and somewhat edible. The briny decay of flesh wafted in the air around the fishmongers.

Gah! I cupped my hand over my nose, rushing past their stands.

My sandals slapped puddles on the sidewalk. Rain slobbered on my legs, making them slick and cold, sending shivers across my skin. I skittered around a group of slow-moving tourists, cursing Afton for insisting I get up early and wear a skirt today.

Finally breaking through the crowd, I charged up the street to the Haymarket entrance to the T.

Under a black umbrella across the street, a beautiful girl with cocoa skin and dark curls huddled next to a guy with equally dark hair and an olive complexion—my two best friends. Nick held the handle while Afton leaned against him to avoid getting wet. Nick's full-face smile told me he enjoyed sharing an umbrella with her.

"Hey, Gia!" Afton yelled over the swooshing of tires across the wet pavement and the insistent honking of aggravated motorists.

I waited for the traffic to clear, missing several opportunities to cross the street. I swallowed hard and took a step down. *You can do this, Gia. No one is going to run you over. Intentionally.* A car turned onto the street, and I quickly hopped back onto the curb. I'd never gotten over my old fears. When the street cleared enough for an elderly person to cross in a walker, I wiped my clammy palms on my skirt and sprinted to the center of the street.

"You have to get over your phobia," Nick called to me. "You live in Boston! Traffic is everywhere!"

"It's okay!" Afton elbowed Nick. "Take your time!"

I took a deep breath and raced across to them.

"Nice. I'm impressed. You actually wore a skirt instead of jeans," Nick said, inspecting my bare legs.

My face warmed. "Wait. Did you just give me a compliment?"

"Well, except..." He hesitated. "You walk like a boy."

"Never mind him. With legs like that, it doesn't

matter how you walk. Come on." Afton hooked her arm around mine. "I can't wait for you to see the Athenæum. It's so amazing. You're going to love it."

I groaned and let her drag me down the steps after Nick. "I'd probably love it just as much later in the day."

As we approached the platform, the train squealed to a stop. We squeezed into its belly with the other passengers and then grasped the nearest bars as the car jolted down the rails. Several minutes later, the train coasted into the Park Street Station. We followed the flow of people up the stairs and to the Boston Common, stopping in Afton's favorite café for lattes and scones. Lost in gossip and our plans for the summer, nearly two hours went by before we headed for the library.

When we reached Beacon Street, excitement—or maybe the two cups of coffee I had downed before leaving the café—hit me. We weren't going to just any library. We were going to the Boston Athenæum, an exclusive library with a pricey annual fee. Afton's father got her a membership at the start of summer. It's a good thing her membership allows tagalongs, since my pop would never splurge like that, not when the public library is free. Which I didn't get, because it wasn't that expensive and would totally be worth it.

"We're here," Afton said. "Ten and a half Beacon Street. Isn't it beautiful? The facade is Neoclassical."

I glanced up at the building. The library walls, which were more than two hundred years old, held tons of history. Nathaniel Hawthorne swore he saw a ghost here once, which I think he probably made up, since he was such a skilled storyteller. "Yeah, it is. Didn't you sketch this building?"

"I did." She bumped me with her shoulder. "I didn't think you actually paid attention to my drawings."

"Well, I do."

Nick pushed open the crimson door to the private realm of the Athenæum, and I chased Afton and Nick up the white marble steps and into the vestibule. Afton showed her membership card at the reception desk. I removed my notebook and pencil from my messenger bag before we dropped it, Afton's purse, and our umbrellas off at the coat check.

Pliable brown linoleum floors muffled our footsteps into the exhibit room. A tiny elevator from another era carried us to an upper level of the library, where bookcases brimming with leather-bound books stood against every wall.

Overhead, more bookcases nested in balconies behind lattice railings. The place dripped with cornices and embellishments. Sweeping ceilings and large windows gave the library an open feel. Every wall held artwork, and antique treasures rested in each corner. It was a library lover's dream, rich with history. My dream.

A memory grabbed my heart. I was about eight and missing my mother, and Nana Kearns took me to a library. She'd said, "Gia, you can never be lonely in the company of books." I wished Nana were here to experience this with me.

"Did you know they have George Washington's personal library here?" Afton's voice pulled me from my thoughts.

"No. I wonder where they keep it," I said.

Nick gaped at a naked sculpture of Venus. "Locked up somewhere, I guess."

The clapping of my sandals against my heels echoed in the quiet, and I winced at each smack. Nick snorted while trying to stifle a laugh. I glared at him. "Quit it."

"Shhh," Afton hissed.

We shuffled into a reading room with forest green walls. Several busts of famous men balancing on white pedestals surrounded the area. A snobby-looking girl with straight blond hair sat at one of the large walnut tables in the middle of the room, tapping a pencil against the surface as she read a book.

"Prada," Afton said.

I gave her a puzzled look. "What?"

"Her sandals. And the watch on her wrist... Coach."

I took her word on that because I wouldn't know designer stuff if it hit me on the head.

Nick's gaze flicked over the girl. "This is cool. I think I'll stay here."

"Whatever." Afton glared at Nick's back. "We're going exploring. When you're finished gawking, come find us."

"Okay," Nick said, clearly distracted, sneaking looks at the girl.

I slid my feet across the floor to the elevators, trying to avoid the dreaded clap of rubber. "Are you okay?"

"I'm fine." By the tone in Afton's voice, I suspected she didn't like Nick ditching us.

"At least we get some girl time," I said.

I must have sounded a little too peppy, because she rolled her eyes at me. She pushed the down button on the elevator. "Yeah, I can give you the tour before we get to work. The Children's Library has some cool stuff in it."

I didn't see the point of riding an elevator when you could get some exercise in. "We could take the stairs. You know, cardio?"

"How about *no*. My feet are killing me in these heels." The doors slid open, and we stepped inside. "Did you know there's a book here bound in human skin?"

"No. Really?" The elevator dropped and my stomach slumped.

Afton removed her sweater and then draped it over her arm. "Really. I saw it."

"No thanks."

"You can't tell it's actual skin," she said. "They treat it or dye it or something, silly."

"I bet they *die* it." The doors rattled apart. There was a slight bounce as we exited the elevator, and I clutched the doorframe. The corner of Afton's lip rose slightly, and I knew her mood was improving. I released my death grip on the frame then followed her into the hallway. "Besides, isn't it illegal or something?"

"Well, the book is from the nineteenth century." Afton shrugged a shoulder. "Who knows what was legal back then?"

"Why would they even do that?" This entire conversation was making *my* skin crawl.

"It's a confession from a thief. Before he died, he requested his own skin be used for the book's cover." The spaghetti strap on Afton's sundress fell down her arm, exposing part of her lacey bra, and she slipped it back in place.

A thirty-something guy passing us gaped, then averted his eyes and hurried his steps, probably realizing Afton's underage status. I rolled my eyes at him. *Jeesh.* Every single move Afton made was sexy. Nick was right. I walked like a guy. I leaned into her side. "Did you just see that perv check you out?"

"Oh, really?" She looked over her shoulder. "He's not all that bad for an older man."

Ugh. "You seriously need a therapist. He's almost Pop's age."

She laughed, grabbed my arm, and turned on her scary narrator voice. "They say this library is haunted."

"Stop it. Are you trying to freak me out?"

She snickered. "You're such a baby."

We stepped into the Children's Library and stopped in the center of the room. A massive light fixture designed to resemble the solar system dominated the ceiling. The hushed rumble of two male voices came from one of the reading nooks. I crossed the room, paused at the built-in aquarium, and inspected the fish. Afton halted beside me.

"This is great," I whispered, not wanting to disturb whoever was in there with us. "Fish and books. What's not to love?" Spotting a sign referencing classic books, I searched the shelves for my all-time favorite novel.

The male voices stopped and there was movement on the other side of the bookcase. I paused to listen, and when the voices started up again, I continued my hunt.

Warmth rushed over me when I found *The Secret Garden*. With its aged green cover, it was the same edition I remembered reading as a young girl. The illustrations inside were beautiful, and I just had to show them to

Afton. Coming around the corner of the case, a little too fast for being in a library, I bumped into a guy dressed in leather biker gear. My book and notebook fell and slapped against the floor.

"Oh, I'm so sorry—" I lost all train of thought at the sight of him. He was gorgeous with tousled brown hair and dark eyes. Tall. He flashed me a crooked smile, a hint of dimples forming in his cheeks, before bending over and picking up my forgotten book.

He held the book out to me. *"Mistress Mary, quite contrary, how does your garden grow?"* He'd quoted a verse from *The Secret Garden* with a sexy accent that tickled my ears.

I stood there like an idiot, my heart pounding hard against my chest, unable to think of a response. The fact that he had read the book and could recite a line from it stunned me. And impressed me.

Say something. Anything.

"Good read there," he said when it was obvious I wasn't going to speak. He winked and nodded to a guy behind him before ambling off. When he reached the end of the row, he paused and glanced back at me, flashing me another killer smile, and then he disappeared around the bookcase.

Tingles rose in my stomach. *He looked back at me.*

The guy following his Royal Hotness gave me a final appraisal before departing. His stringy blond hair hung over his large forehead. It looked like he hadn't washed it in weeks, and there was probably an acne breeding ground under it. He grinned, and I broke eye contact with him, making for the nearest window.

Oh God, you're so lame, Gia. You could have finished the quote or anything less tragic than not speaking at all. The response I would have said played in my head. *With silver bells, and cockleshells, and marigolds all in a row.* Why? Why hadn't I said that?

The window overlooked the Granary Burying Grounds. I hugged my books to my chest and spoke to Afton's reflection in the windowpane, listening to the guys' boots retreating from the room, not daring to sneak a look. "I've been to that graveyard before. Mother Goose is buried there."

She strained her neck forward to view the tombstones below.

I shifted to face her. "Did you see that guy? He was— he was—" I was still at a loss for words.

"Probably European by the sound of his accent," she said, her eyes shifting over the tourists weaving around the gravestones below. "The taller one is delicious, though."

"I know, and I just stood there. He talked to me, and I just stood there."

"Well, maybe you'll see him again." Her outlook was always positive.

I sagged against the window frame. "I'd probably make a fool of myself again."

"I don't get the appeal," she said, squinting out the window then straightening. "It's just a bunch of old stones etched with names you can hardly read."

I feigned a shocked expression. "It's history. Sam Adams and Paul Revere are buried there."

"Don't you get enough history in school?"

"Never. I could walk in it all day."

We sat at one of the tables, flipping through picture books. It was Afton's favorite thing to do at libraries. The illustrations inspired her art.

Afton sighed. "I'm hungry. Let's get some lunch."

We grabbed our bags from the coat check and texted Nick. He told us to go without him. Afton and I gave each other puzzled looks. He never refused food. We downed lemonades and pretzels on the Common then returned to the Athenæum. I sent a message to Nick that we were back before checking in my bag.

After Afton dragged me on a tour from breathtaking rooms framed by towering bookcases and soaring windows to a balconied patio, we rode one of the small elevators to the fifth-floor reading room. Except for a few patrons, the area was vacant. We found the books we needed for Afton's and Nick's summer projects and then settled at one of the tables in the middle of the room. The sucky part about going to a private school was that each summer we had to write an essay over the break. Since I hated having to-do lists hanging over my head, I'd finished mine already.

"Mint?" Afton extended a tin while flipping through a small textbook on Crispus Attucks, an African-American minuteman shot during the Boston Massacre.

"Sure. Thanks." I grabbed one then popped it into my mouth. After flipping my notebook open, I readied my pencil to make notes on Samuel Adams for Nick.

The guy I'd bumped into in the children's area strutted to a table across the room from us, carrying a large book. He stood out in the conservative atmosphere of the library with his messy hair and tight leather outfit clinging to his toned body. In an easy movement, he sat down and started thumbing through the volume.

From our table, I snuck glances at him. He ran his hand through his tousled hair as he studied the pages, and I couldn't look away. It was like everyone in the room vanished; every sexy movement he made was choreographed just for me.

His gaze snapped up, catching mine.

Busted. I choked on my breath mint.

His intense stare held me for several seconds before the corner of his lips curved up, and his dimples made an appearance. I cleared my throat. The mint sliding down my esophagus was somewhat painful.

Okay, stop staring and do something. I gave him a bright smile, fumbling my pencil in my trembling fingers until it dropped. His eyes sparked with amusement, and he nodded at me.

"Shhhh," Afton said in response to the pencil clattering against the table.

I glanced at her. Focused on her book, a strand of her dark hair twisted around her finger, she hadn't even noticed him. A gust of air came from the guy's direction and rustled her hair. I looked back at him. The pages of his book fluttered, and then settled back in place.

He was gone.